THE
YUKON TRAIL

Center Point
Large Print

Also by William MacLeod Raine and available from Center Point Large Print:

Gunsmoke Trail
The Trail of Danger
Square-Shooter
This Nettle Danger
Saddlebum
Robber's Roost
Roads of Doubt
Trail's End

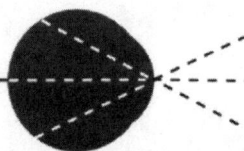

**This Large Print Book carries the
Seal of Approval of N.A.V.H.**

THE YUKON TRAIL

William MacLeod Raine

CENTER POINT LARGE PRINT
THORNDIKE, MAINE

This Center Point Large Print edition
is published in the year 2021 by arrangement with
Golden West Literary Agency.

Originally published in the US by Houghton Mifflin.
Originally published in the UK by Jerrolds.

The text of this Large Print edition is unabridged.
In other aspects, this book may vary
from the original edition.
Printed in the United States of America
on permanent paper.
Set in 16-point Times New Roman type.

ISBN: 978-1-64358-782-0 (hardcover)
ISBN: 978-1-64358-786-8 (paperback)

The Library of Congress has cataloged this record under
Library of Congress Control Number: 2020946370

TO
MY BROTHER

EDGAR C. RAINE

who knew the Lights of Dawson when
they were a magnet to the feet of those
answering the call of Adventure,
who mushed the Yukon Trail from
its headwaters to Bering Sea,
who still finds in the Frozen North
the Romance of the Last Frontier.

CHAPTER I
GOING "IN"

The midnight sun had set, but in a crotch between two snow-peaks it had kindled a vast caldron from which rose a mist of jewels, garnet and turquoise, topaz and amethyst and opal, all swimming in a sea of molten gold. The glow of it still clung to the face of the broad Yukon, as a flush does to the soft, wrinkled cheek of a girl just roused from deep sleep.

Except for a faint murkiness in the air it was still day. There was light enough for the four men playing pinochle on the upper deck, though the women of their party, gossiping in chairs grouped near at hand, had at last put aside their embroidery. The girl who sat by herself at a little distance held a magazine still open on her lap. If she were not reading, her attitude suggested it was less because of the dusk than that she had surrendered herself to the spell of the mysterious beauty which for this hour at least had transfigured the North to a land all light and atmosphere and color.

Gordon Elliot had taken the boat at Pierre's Portage, fifty miles farther down the river. He had come direct from the creeks, and his impressions

7

of the motley pioneer life at the gold-diggings were so vivid that he had found an isolated corner of the deck where he could scribble them in a notebook while still fresh.

But he had not been too busy to see that the girl in the wicker chair was as much of an outsider as he was. Plainly this was her first trip in. Gordon was a stranger in the Yukon country, one not likely to be over-welcome when it became known what his mission was. It may have been because he was out of the picture himself that he resented a little the exclusion of the young woman with the magazine. Certainly she herself gave no evidence of feeling about it. Her long-lashed eyes looked dreamily across the river to the glowing hills beyond. Not once did they turn with any show of interest to the lively party under the awning.

From where he was leaning against the deck-house Elliot could see only a fine, chiseled profile shading into a mass of crisp, black hair, but some quality in the detachment of her personality stimulated gently his imagination. He wondered who she could be. His work had taken him to frontier camps before, but he could not place her as a type. The best he could do was to guess that she might be the daughter of some territorial official on her way in to join him.

A short, thick-set man who had ridden down on the stage with Elliot to Pierre's Portage drifted along the deck toward him. He wore the careless garb of a mining man in a country which looks first to comfort.

"Bound for Kusiak?" he asked, by way of opening conversation.

"Yes," answered Gordon.

The miner nodded toward the group under the awning. "That bunch lives at Kusiak. They've got on at different places the last two or three days—except Selfridge and his wife, they've been out. Gucss you can tell that from hearing her talk—the little woman in red with the snappy black eyes. She's spillin' over with talk about the styles in New York and the cabarets and the new shows. That pot-bellied little fellow in the checked suit is Selfridge. He is Colby Macdonald's man Friday."

Elliot took in with a quickened interest the group bound for Kusiak. He had noticed that they monopolized as a matter of course the best places on the deck and in the dining-room. They were civil enough to outsiders, but their manner had the unconscious selfishness that often regulates social activities. It excluded from their gayety everybody that did not belong to the proper set.

"That sort of thing gets my goat," the miner went on sourly. "Those women over there have elected themselves Society with a capital S. They put on all the airs the Four Hundred do in New York. And who the hell are they anyhow?—wives to a bunch of grafting politicians mostly."

9

From the casual talk that had floated to him, with its many little allusions punctuating the jolly give-and-take of their repartee, Elliot guessed that their lives had the same background of tennis, dinners, hops, official gossip, and business. They evidently knew one another with the intimacy that comes only to the segment of a small community shut off largely from the world and forced into close social relations. No doubt they had loaned each other money occasionally, stood by in trouble, and gossiped back and forth about their shortcomings and family skeletons even as society on the outside does.

"That's the way of the world, isn't it? Our civilization is built on the group system," suggested Elliot.

"Maybeso," grumbled the miner. "But I hate to see Alaska come to it. Me, I saw this country first in '97—packed an outfit in over the Pass. Every man stood on his own hind legs then. He got there if he was strong—mebbe; he bogged down on the trail good and plenty if he was weak. We didn't have any of the artificial stuff then. A man had to have the guts to stand the gaff."

"I suppose it was a wild country, Mr. Strong."

The little miner's eyes gleamed. "Best country in the world. We didn't stand for anything that wasn't on the level. It was a poor man's country—wages fifteen dollars a day and plenty of work. Everybody had a chance. Anybody could stake a claim and gamble on his luck. Now the big corporations have slipped in and grabbed the best. It ain't a prospector's proposition any more. Instead of faro banks we've got savings banks. The wide-open dance hall has quit business in favor of moving pictures. And, as I said before, we've got Society."

"All frontier countries have to come to it."

"Hmp! In the days I'm telling you about that crowd there couldn't 'a' hustled meat to fill their bellies three meals. Parasites, that's what they are. They're living off that bunch of roughnecks down there and folks like 'em."

With a wave of his hand Strong pointed to a group of miners who had boarded the boat with them at Pierre's Portage. There were about a dozen of the men, for the most part husky, heavy-set foreigners. They had been drinking, and were in a sullen humor. Elliot gathered from their talk that they had lost their jobs because they had tried to organize an incipient strike in the Frozen Gulch district.

"Roughnecks and booze-fighters—that's all they are. But they earn their way. Not that I blame Macdonald for firing them, mind you," continued the miner.

"Were they working for Macdonald?"

"Yep. His superintendent up there was too soft. These here Swedes got gay. Mac hit the trail for Frozen Gulch. He hammered his big fist into the bread-basket of the ringleader and said, 'Git!' That fellow's running yet, I'll bet. Then Mac called the men together and read the riot act to them. He fired this bunch on the boat and was out of the camp before you could bat an eye. It was the cleanest hurry-up job I ever did see."

"From what I've heard about him he must be a remarkable man."

"He's the biggest man in Alaska, bar none."

This was a subject that interested Gordon Elliot very much. Colby Macdonald and his activities had brought him to the country.

"Do you mean personally—or because he represents the big corporations?"

"Both. His word comes pretty near being law up here, not only because he stands for the Consolidated, but because he's one man from the ground up. I ain't any too strong for that New York bunch of capitalists back of Mac, but I've got to give it to him that he's all there without leaning on anybody."

"I've heard that he's a domineering man—rides roughshod over others. Is that right, Mr. Strong?"

"He's a bear for getting his own way," grinned the little miner. "If you won't get out of his road he peels your hide off and hangs it up to dry. But I can't help liking him. He's big every way you take him. He'll stand the acid, Mac will."

"Do you mean that he's square—honest?"

"You've said two things, my friend," answered Strong dryly. "He's square. If he tells you anything, don't worry because he ain't put down his John Hancock before a notary. He'll see it through to a finish—to a fighting finish if he has to. Don't waste any time looking for fat or yellow streaks in Mac. They ain't there. Nobody ever heard him squeal yet and what's more nobody ever will."

"No wonder men like him."

"But when you say honest—Hell, no! Not the way you define honesty down in the States. He's a grabber, Mac is. Better not leave anything valuable around unless you've got it spiked to the floor. He takes what he wants."

"What does he look like?" asked Gordon.

"Oh, I don't know." Strong hesitated, while he searched for words to show the picture in his mind. "Big as a house—steps out like a buck in the spring—blue-gray eyes that bore right through you."

"How old?"

"Search me. You never think of age when you're looking at him. Forty-five, mebbe—or fifty—I don't know."

"Married?"

"No-o." Hanford Strong nodded in the direction of the Kusiak circle. "They say he's going to marry Mrs. Mallory. She's the one with the red hair."

It struck young Elliot that the miner was dismissing Mrs. Mallory in too cavalier a fashion. She was the sort of woman at whom men look twice, and then continue to look while she appears magnificently unaware of it. Her hair was not red, but of a lustrous bronze, amazingly abundant, and dressed in waves with the careful skill of a coiffeur. Half-shut, smouldering eyes had met his for an instant at dinner across the table and had told him she was a woman subtle and complex. Slightest shades of meaning she could convey with a lift of the eyebrow or an intonation of the musical voice. If she was already fencing with the encroaching years there was little evidence of it in her opulent good looks. She had manifestly specialized in graceful idleness and was prepared to meet with superb confidence the competition of débutantes. The elusive shadow of lost illusions, of knowledge born of experience, was the only betrayal of vanished youth in her equipment.

CHAPTER II
ENTER A MAN

The whistle of the Hannah blew for the Tatlah Cache landing while Strong and Elliot were talking. Wally Selfridge had just bid three hundred seventy and found no help in the widow. He pushed toward each of the other players one red chip and two white ones.

"Can't make it," he announced. "I needed a jack of clubs."

The men counted their chips and settled up in time to reach the deck rail just as the gangplank was thrown out to the wharf. The crew transferred to the landing a pouch of mail, half a ton of sacked potatoes, some mining machinery, and several boxes containing provisions and dry goods.

A man came to the end of the wharf carrying a suitcase. He was well-set, thick in the chest, and broad-shouldered. He came up the gangplank with the strong, firm tread of a man in his prime. Looking down from above, Gordon Elliot guessed him to be in the early thirties.

Mrs. Mallory was the first to recognize him, which she did with a drawling little shout of welcome. "Oh you, Mr. Man. I knew you first. I speak for you," she cried.

15

The man on the gangplank looked up, smiled, and lifted to her his broad gray Stetson in a wave of greeting.

"How do you do, Mrs. Mallory? Glad to see you."

The miners from Frozen Gulch were grouped together on the lower deck. At sight of the man with the suitcase a sullen murmur rose among them. Those in the rear pushed forward and closed the lane leading to the cabins. One of the miners was flung roughly against the new passenger. With a wide, powerful sweep of his arm the man who had just come aboard hurled the miner back among his companions.

"Gangway!" he said brusquely, and as he strode forward did not even glance in the direction of the angry men pressing toward him.

"Here. Keep back there, you fellows. None of that rough stuff goes," ordered the mate sharply.

The big Cornishman who had been tossed aside crouched for a spring. He launched himself forward with the awkward force of a bear. The suitcase described a whirling arc of a circle with the arm of its owner as the radius. The bag and the head of the miner came into swift impact. Like a bullock which has been pole-axed the man went to the floor. He turned over with a groan and lay still.

The new passenger looked across the huge, sprawling body at the group of miners facing him. They glared in savage hate. All they needed was a leader to send them driving at him with the force of an avalanche. The man at whom they raged did not give an inch. He leaned forward slightly, his weight resting on the balls of his feet, alert to the finger tips. But in his eyes a grim little smile of derisive amusement rested.

"Next," he taunted.

Then the mate got busy. He hustled his stevedores forward in front of the miners and shook his fist in their faces as he stormed up and down. If they wanted trouble, by God! it was waiting for 'em, he swore in apoplectic fury. The Hannah was a river boat and not a dive for wharf rats. No bunch of roughnecks could come aboard a boat where he was mate and start anything. They could not assault any passengers of his and make it stick.

The man with the suitcase did not wait to hear out his tirade. He followed the purser to his stateroom, dropped his baggage beside the berth, and joined the Kusiak group on the upper deck.

They greeted him eagerly, a little effusively, as if they were anxious to prove themselves on good terms with him. The deference they paid and his assured acceptance of it showed him to be a man of importance. But apart from other considerations, he dominated by mental and physical virility the circle of which he instantly became the center. Only Mrs. Mallory held her own, and even she showed a quickened interest. Her indolent, half-disdainful manner sheathed a soft sensuousness that held the provocation of sex appeal.

"What was the matter?" asked Selfridge. "How did the trouble start?"

The big man shrugged his shoulders. "It didn't start. Some of the outfit thought they were looking for a row, but they balked on the job when Trelawney got his." Turning to Mrs. Mallory, he changed the subject abruptly. "Did you have a good time down the river?"

Gordon, as he watched from a little distance, corrected earlier impressions. This man had passed the thirties. Salt and pepper sprinkled the temples of his strong, lean head. He had the thick neck and solid trunk of middle life, but he carried himself so superbly that his whole bearing denied that years could touch his splendid physique. The suit he wore was a wrinkled corduroy, with trouser legs thrust into high-laced boots. An outdoor tan had been painted upon his face and neck, from the point where the soft flannel shirt fell away to show the fine slope of the throat line to the shoulders.

Strong had stepped to the wharf to talk with an old acquaintance, but when the boat threw out a warning signal he made a hurried good-bye and came on board. He rejoined Elliot.

"Well, what d'you think of him? Was I right?"

18

The young man had already guessed who this imperious stranger was. "I never saw anybody get away with a hard job as easily as he did that one. You could see with half an eye that those fellows meant fight. They were all primed for it—and he bluffed them out."

"Bluffed them—huh! If that's what you call bluffing. I was where I could see just what happened. Colby Macdonald wasn't even looking at Trelawney, but you bet he saw him start. That suitcase traveled like a streak of light. You'd 'a' thought it weighed about two pounds. That ain't all either. Mac used his brains. Guess what was in that grip."

"The usual thing, I suppose."

"You've got another guess—packed in among his socks and underwear was about twenty pounds of ore samples. The purser told me. It was that quartz put Trelawney to sleep so thorough that he'd just begun to wake up when I passed a minute ago."

The young man turned his eyes again upon the big Canadian Scotchman. He was talking with Mrs. Mallory, who was leaning back luxuriously in a steamer chair she had brought aboard at St. Michael's. It would have been hard to conceive a contrast greater than the one between this pampered heiress of the ages and the modern business berserk who looked down into her mocking eyes. He was the embodiment

19

of the dominant male,—efficient to the last inch of his straight six feet. What he wanted he had always taken, by the sheer strength that was in him. Back of her smiling insolence lay a silken force to match his own. She too had taken what she wanted from life, but she had won it by indirection. Manifestly she was of those women who conceive that charm and beauty are tools to bend men to their wills. Was it the very width of the gulf between them that made the appeal of the clash in the sex duel upon which they had engaged?

The dusky young woman with the magazine was the first of those on the upper deck to retire for the night. She flitted so quietly that Gordon did not notice until she had gone. Mrs. Selfridge and her friends disappeared with their men folks, calling gay good-nights to one another as they left.

Macdonald and Mrs. Mallory still talked. After a time she too vanished.

The big promoter leaned against the deck rail, where he was joined by Selfridge. For a long time they talked in low voices. The little man had most to say. His chief listened, but occasionally interrupted to ask a sharp, incisive question.

Elliot, sitting farther forward with Strong, judged that Selfridge was making a report of his trip. Once he caught a fragment of their talk, enough to confirm this impression.

"Did Winton tell you that himself?" demanded the Scotchman.

The answer of his employee came in a murmur so low that the words were lost. But the name used told Gordon a good deal. The Commissioner of the General Land Office at Washington signed his letters Harold B. Winton.

Strong tossed the stub of his cigarette overboard and nodded good-night. A glance at his watch told Elliot that it was past two o'clock. He rose, stretched, and sauntered back to his stateroom.

The young man had just taken off his coat when there came the hurried rush of trampling feet upon the hurricane deck above. Almost instantly he heard a cry of alarm. Low voices, quick with suppressed excitement, drifted back to him. He could hear the shuffling of footsteps and the sound of heavy bodies moving.

Some one lifted a frightened shout. "Help! Help!" The call had come, he thought, from Selfridge.

Gordon flung open the door of his room, raced along the deck, and took the stairs three at a time. A huddle of men swayed and shifted heavily in front of him. So close was the pack that the motion resembled the writhing of some prehistoric monster rather than the movements of individual human beings. In that half-light tossing arms and legs looked like tentacles flung out in agony by the mammoth reptile. Its progress was jerky and convulsive, sometimes tortuous, but it traveled slowly toward the rail as if by the impulsion of an irresistible pressure.

Even as he ran toward the mass, Elliot noticed that the only sounds were grunts, stertorous breathings, and the scraping of feet. The attackers wanted no publicity. The attacked was too busy to waste breath in futile cries. He was fighting for his life with all the stark energy nature and his ancestors had given him.

Two men, separated from the crowd, lay on the deck farther aft. One was on top of the other, his fingers clutching the gullet of his helpless opponent. The agony of the man underneath found expression only in the drumming heels that beat a tattoo on the floor. The spasmodic feet were shod in Oxford tans of an ultra-fashionable cut. No doubt the owner of the smart footwear had been pulled down as he was escaping to shout the alarm.

The runner hurdled the two in his stride and plunged straight at the struggling tangle. He caught one man by the shoulders from behind and flung him back. He struck hard, smashing blows as he fought his way to the heart of the mêlée. Heavy-fisted miners with corded muscles landed upon his face and head and neck. The strange excitement of the battle lust surged through his veins. He did not care a straw for the odds.

The sudden attack of Elliot had opened the

pack. The man battling against a dozen was Colby Macdonald. The very number of his foes had saved him so far from being rushed overboard or trampled down. In their desire to get at him they hindered each other, struck blows that found the wrong mark. His coat and shirt were in rags. He was bruised and battered and bleeding from the chest up. But he was still slogging hard.

They had him pressed to the rail. A huge miner, head down, had his arms around the waist of the Scotchman and was trying to throw him overboard. Macdonald lashed out and landed flush upon the cheek of a man attempting to brain him with a billet of wood. He hammered home a short-arm jolt against the ear of the giant who was giving him the bear grip.

The big miner grunted, but hung on like a football tackler. With a jerk he raised Macdonald from the floor just as three or four others rushed him again. The rail gave way, splintered like kindling wood. The Scotchman and the man at grips with him went over the side together.

Clear and loud rang the voice of Elliot. "Man overboard!"

The wheelsman had known for some minutes that there was trouble afoot. He signaled to the engine room to reverse and blew short, sharp shrieks of warning. Already deckhands and officers, scantily clad, were appearing from fore and aft.

"Men overboard—two of 'em!" explained Elliot in a shout from the boat which he was trying to lower.

The first mate and another man ran to help him. The three of them lowered and manned the boat. Gordon sat in the bow and gave directions while the other two put their backs into the stroke. Quite casually Elliot noticed that the man in the waist had a purple bruise on his left cheek bone. The young man himself had put it there not three minutes since.

Across the water came a call for help. "I'm sinking—hurry!"

The other man in the river was a dozen yards from the one in distress. With strong, swift, overhand strokes he shot through the water.

"All right," he called presently. "I've got him."

The oarsmen drew alongside the swimmer. With one hand Macdonald caught hold of the edge of the boat. The other clutched the rescued man by the hair of his head.

"Look out. You're drowning him," the mate warned.

"Am I?" Macdonald glanced with mild interest at the head that had been until that moment submerged. "Shows how absent-minded a man gets. I was thinking about how he tried to drown me, I expect."

They dragged the miner aboard.

"Go ahead. I'll swim down," Macdonald ordered.

"Better come aboard," advised the mate.

"No. I'm all right."

The Scotchman pushed himself back from the boat and fell into an easy stroke. Nevertheless, there was power in it, for he reached the Hannah before the rescued miner had been helped to the deck.

A dozen passengers, crowded on the lower deck, pushed forward eagerly to see. Among them was Selfridge, his shirt and collar torn loose at the neck and his immaculate checked suit dusty and disheveled. He was wearing a pair of up-to-date Oxford tans.

The Scotch-Canadian shook himself like a Newfoundland dog. He looked around with sardonic amusement, a grin on his swollen and disfigured face.

"Quite a pleasant welcome home," he said ironically, his cold eyes fixed on a face that looked as if it might have been kicked by a healthy mule. "Eh, Trelawney?"

The Cornishman glared at him, and turned away with a low, savage oath.

"Are you hurt, Mr. Macdonald?" asked the captain.

"Hurt! Not at all, Captain. I cut myself while I was shaving this morning—just a scratch," was the ironic answer.

"There's been some dirty work going on. I'll see the men are punished, sir."

"Forget it, Captain. I'll attend to that little matter." His jaunty, almost insolent glance made the half-circle again. "Sorry you were too late for the party, gentlemen,—most of you. I see three or four of you who were 'among those present.' It was a strictly exclusive affair. And now, if you don't mind, I'll say good-night."

He turned on his heel, went up the stairway to the deck above, and disappeared into his state-room.

The rescued miner, propped against the cabin wall where he had been placed, broke into sudden excited protest. "Ach! He tried to drown me. Mein head—he hold it under the water."

"Ain't that just like a Swede?" retorted the mate in disgust. "Mac saves his life. Then the roughneck kicks because he got a belly full of Yukon. Sure Mac soused him some. Why shouldn't he?"

"I ain't no Swede," explained the big miner sullenly.

The mate did not think it worth his while to explain that "Swede" was merely his generic term of contempt for all foreigners.

CHAPTER III
THE GIRL FROM DROGHEDA

Gordon Elliot was too much of a night owl to be an early riser, but next morning he was awakened by the tramp of hurried feet along the deck to the accompaniment of brusque orders, together with frequent angry puffing and snorting of the boat. From the quiver of the walls he guessed that the Hannah was stuck on a sandbar. The mate's language gave backing to this surmise. Divided in mind between his obligation to the sleeping passengers and his duty to get the boat on her way, that officer spilled a good deal of subdued sulphurous language upon the situation.

"All together now. Get your back into it. Why are you running around like a chicken without a head, Reeves?" he snapped.

Evidently the deck hands were working to get the Hannah off by poling.

Elliot tried to settle back to sleep, but after two or three ineffectual efforts gave it up. He rose and did one or two setting-up exercises to limber his joints. The first of these flashed the signal to his brain that he was stiff and sore. This brought to mind the fight on the hurricane deck, and he smiled. His face was about as mobile as if it were

27

in a plaster cast. It hurt every time he twitched a muscle.

The young man stepped to the looking-glass. Both eyes were blacked, his lip had been cut, and there was a purple weal well up on his left cheek. He stopped himself from grinning only just in time to save another twinge of pain.

"Some party while it lasted. I never saw more willing mixers. Everybody seemed anxious to sit in except Mr. Wally Selfridge," he explained to his reflection. "But Macdonald is the class. He's there with both right and left. That uppercut of his is vicious. Don't ever get in the way of it, Gordon Elliot." He examined his injuries more closely in the glass. "Some one landed a peach on my right lamp and the other is in mourning out of sympathy. Oh, well, I ain't the only prize beauty on board this morning." The young man forgot and smiled. "Ouch! Don't do that, Gordon. Yes, son. 'There's many a black, black eye, they say, but none so bright as mine.' Now isn't that the truth?"

He bathed, dressed, and went out on the deck.

Early though he was, one passenger at least was up before him. The young woman he had noticed last evening with the magazine was doing a constitutional. A slight breeze was stirring, and as she moved against it the white skirt clung first to one knee and then the other, moulding itself to the long lines of her limbs with exquisite grace of motion. It was as though her walk were the expression of a gallant and buoyant personality.

Irish he guessed her when the deep-blue eyes rested on his for an instant as she passed, and fortified his conjecture by the coloring of the clear-skinned face and the marks of the Celtic race delicately stamped upon it.

The purser came out of his room and joined Elliot. He smiled at sight of the young man's face.

"Your map's a little out of plumb this morning, sir," he ventured.

"But you ought to see the other fellow," came back Gordon boyishly.

"I've seen him—several of him. We've got the best collection of bruises on board I ever clapped eyes on. I've got to give it to you and Mr. Macdonald. You know how to hit."

"Oh, I'm not in his class."

Gordon Elliot meant what he said. He was himself an athlete, had played for three years left tackle on his college eleven. More than one critic had picked him for the All-America team. He could do his hundred in just a little worse than ten seconds. But after all he was a product of training and of the gymnasiums. Macdonald was what nature and a long line of fighting Highland ancestors had made him. His sinewy, knotted strength, his massive build, the breadth of shoulder and depth of chest—mushing on long snow trails

29

was the gymnasium that had contributed to these.

The purser chuckled. "He's a good un, Mac is. They say he liked to have drowned Northrup after he had saved him."

Elliot was again following with his eyes the lilt of the girl's movements. Apparently he had not heard what the officer said. At least he gave no answer.

With a grin the purser opened another attack. "Don't blame you a bit, Mr. Elliot. She's the prettiest colleen that ever sailed from Dublin Bay."

The young man brought his eyes home. They answered engagingly the smile of the purser.

"Who is she?"

"The name on the books is Sheba O'Neill."

"From Dublin, you say."

"Oh, if you want to be literal, her baggage says Drogheda. Ireland is Ireland to me."

"Where is she bound for?"

"Kusiak."

The young woman passed them with a little nod of morning greeting to the purser. Fine and dainty though she was, Miss O'Neill gave an impression of radiant strength.

"Been with you all the way up the river?" asked Elliot after she had passed.

"Yep. She came up on the Skagit from Seattle."

"What is she going to do at Kusiak?"

Again the purser grinned. "What do they all do—the good-looking ones?"

"Get married, you mean?"

"Surest thing you know. Girls coming up ask me what to bring by way of outfit. I used to make out a long list. Now I tell them to bring clothes enough for six weeks and their favorite wedding march."

"Is this girl engaged?"

"Can't prove it by me," said the officer lightly. "But she'll never get out of Alaska a spinster—not that girl. She may be going in to teach, or to run a millinery store, or to keep books for a trading company. She'll stay to bring up kiddies of her own. They all do."

Three children came up the stairway, caught sight of Miss O'Neill, and raced pell-mell across the deck to her.

The young woman's face was transformed. It was bubbling with tenderness, with gay and happy laughter. Flinging her arms wide, she waited for them. With incoherent cries of delight they flung themselves upon her. Her arms enveloped all three as she stooped for their hugs and kisses.

The two oldest were girls. The youngest was a fat, cuddly little boy with dimples in his soft cheeks.

"I dwessed myself, Aunt Sheba. Didn't I, Gwen?"

"Not all by yourself, Billie?" inquired the Irish girl, registering a proper amazement.

31

He nodded his head slowly and solemnly up and down. "Honeth to goodness."

Sheba stooped and held him off to admire. "All by yourself—just think of that."

"We helped just the teeniest bit on the buttons," confessed Janet, the oldest of the small family.

"And I tied his shoes," added Gwendolen, "after he had laced them."

"Billie will be such a big man Daddie won't know him." And Sheba gave him another hug.

Gwendolen snuggled close to Miss O'Neill. "You always smell so sweet and clean and violety, Aunt Sheba," she whispered in confidence.

"You're spoiling me, Gwen," laughed the young woman. "You've kissed the blarney stone. It's a good thing you're leaving the boat to-day."

Miss Gwen had one more confidence to make in the ear of her friend. "I wish you'd come too and be our new mamma," she begged.

A shell-pink tinge crept into the milky skin of the Irish girl. She was less sure of herself, more easily embarrassed, than the average American of her age and sex. Occasionally in her manner was that effect of shyness one finds in the British even after they have escaped from provincialism.

"Are all your things gathered ready for packing, Janet?" she asked quietly.

The purser gave information to Elliot. "They call her Aunt Sheba, but she's no relative of theirs. The kids are on their way in to their father, who is an engineer on one of the creeks back of Katma. Their mother died two months ago. Miss O'Neill met them first aboard the Skagit on the way up and she has mothered them ever since. Some women are that way, bless 'em. I know because I've been married to one myself six months. She's back there at St. Michael's, and she just grabs at every baby in the block."

The eyes of Elliot rested on Miss O'Neill. "She loves children."

"She sure does—no bluff about that." An imp of mischief sparkled in the eye of the supercargo. "Not married yourself, are you, Mr. Elliot?"

"No."

"Hmp!"

That was all he said, but Gordon felt the blood creep into his face. This annoyed him, so he added brusquely,—

"And not likely to be."

When the call for breakfast came Miss O'Neill took her retinue of youngsters with her to the dining-room. Looking across from his seat at an adjoining table, Elliot could see her waiting upon them with a fine absorption in their needs. She prepared an orange for Billie and offered to the little girls suggestions as to ordering that were accepted by them as a matter of course. Unconsciously the children recognized in her the eternal Mother.

Before they had been long in the dining-room

Macdonald came in carrying a sheaf of business papers. He glanced around, recognized Elliot, and made instantly for the seat across the table from him. On his face and head were many marks of the recent battle.

"Trade you a cauliflower ear for a pair of black eyes, Mr. Elliot," he laughed as he shook hands with the man whose name he had just learned from the purser.

The grip of his brown, muscular hand was strong. It was in character with the steady, cool eyes set deep beneath the jutting forehead, with the confident carriage of the deep, broad shoulders. He looked a dynamic American, who trod the way of the forceful and fought for his share of the spoils.

"You might throw in several other little souvenirs to boot and not miss them," suggested Elliot with a smile.

Macdonald nodded indifferently. "I gave and I took, which was as it should be. But it's different with you, Mr. Elliot. This wasn't your row."

"I hadn't been in a good mix-up since I left college. It did me a lot of good."

"Much obliged, anyhow." He turned his attention to a lady entering the dining-room. " 'Mornin', Mrs. Selfridge. How's Wally?"

She threw up her hands in despair. "He's on his second bottle of liniment already. I expect those ruffians have ruined his singing voice. It's a mercy they didn't murder both him and you, Mr. Macdonald. When I think of how close you both came to death last night—"

"I don't know about Wally, but I had no notion of dying, Mrs. Selfridge. They mussed us up a bit. That was all."

"But they *meant* to kill you, the cowards. And they almost did it too. Look at Wally—confined to his bed and speaking in a whisper. Look at you—a wreck, horribly beaten up, almost drowned. We must drive the villains out of the country or send them to prison."

Mrs. Selfridge always talked in superlatives. She had an enthusiasm for the dramatics of conversation. Her supple hands, her shrill, eager voice, the snapping black eyes, all had the effect of startling headlines to the story she might be telling.

"Am I a wreck?" the big Scotchman wanted to know. "I feel as husky as a well-fed malamute."

"Oh, you *talk*. But we all know you—how brave and strong you are. That's why this outrage ought to be punished. What would Alaska do if anything happened to you?"

"I hadn't thought of that," admitted Macdonald. "The North would have to go out of business, I suppose. But you're right about one thing, Mrs. Selfridge. I'm brave and strong enough at the breakfast table. Steward, will you bring me a double order of these shirred eggs—and a small steak?"

"Well, I'm glad you can still joke, Mr. Macdonald, after such a terrible experience. All I can say is that I hope Wally isn't permanently injured. He hasn't your fine constitution, and one never can tell about internal injuries." Mrs. Selfridge sighed and passed to her place.

The eyes of the big man twinkled. "Our little fracas has been a godsend to Mrs. Selfridge. Wally and I will both emerge as heroes of a desperate struggle. You won't even get a mention. But it's a pity about Wally's injuries—and his singing voice."

The younger man agreed with a gravity back of which his amusement was apparent. The share of Selfridge in the battle had been limited to leg work only, but this had not been good enough to keep him from being overhauled and having his throat squeezed.

Elliot finished breakfast first and left Macdonald looking over a long typewritten document. He had it propped against a water-bottle and was reading as he ate. The paper was a report Selfridge had brought in to him from a clerk in the General Land Office. The big Canadian and the men he represented were dealing directly with the heads of the Government departments, but they thought it the part of wisdom to keep in their employ subordinates in the capacity of secret service agents to spy upon the higher-ups.

CHAPTER IV
THE CREVASSE

For an hour before the Hannah readied Katma Miss O'Neill was busy getting her little brood ready. In that last half-day she was a creature of moods to them. They, too, like Sheba herself, were adventuring into a new world. Somehow they represented to her the last tie that bound her to the life she was leaving. Her heart was tender as a Madonna to these lambs so ill-fitted to face a frigid waste. Their mother had been a good woman. She could tell that. But she had no way of knowing what kind of man their father might be.

Sheba gave Janet advice about where to keep her money and when to wear rubbers and what to do for Billie's cold. She put up a lunch for them to take on the stage. When they said their sniffling good-byes at Katma she was suspiciously bright and merry. Soon the children were laughing again with her.

One glance at their father, who introduced himself to Miss O'Neill as John Husted, relieved her mind greatly. His spontaneous delight at seeing them again and his choking gratitude to her for having looked after them were evidence enough that this kind-eyed man meant to be both father and mother to his recovered little folks. His emotion was too poignant for him to talk about his wife, but Sheba understood and liked him better for it.

Her temporary family stood on the end of the wharf and called good-byes to the girl.

"Tum soon and see us, Aunt Sheba," Billie shouted from his seat on the shoulder of his father.

The children waved handkerchiefs as long as she could be distinguished by them. When they turned away she went directly to her room.

Elliot was passing forward when Miss O'Neill opened her stateroom door to go in. The eyes of the young woman were blind with tears and she was biting her lip to keep back the emotion that welled up. He knew she was very fond of the motherless children, but he guessed at an additional reason for her sobs. She too was as untaught as a child in the life of this frontier land. Whatever she found here—how much of hard-ship or happiness, of grief or woe—she knew that she had left behind forever the safe harborage of quiet waters in which her life craft had always floated.

It came on to rain in the afternoon. Heavy clouds swept across from the mountains, and the sodden sky opened like a sluice-box. The Kusiak contingent, driven indoors, resorted to bridge

Miss O'Neill read. Gordon Elliot wrote letters, dawdled over magazines, and lounged alternately in the ladies' parlor and the smoking-room, where Macdonald, Strong, a hardware merchant from Fairbanks, and a pair of sour-dough miners had settled themselves to a poker game that was to last all night and well into the next day.

Of the two bridge tables all the players were old-timers except Mrs. Mallory. Most of them were young enough in years, but they had been of the North long enough to know the gossip of the country and its small politics intimately. They shared common hopes of the day when Alaska would be thrown open to industry and a large population.

But Mrs. Mallory had come in over the ice for the first time last winter. The other women felt that she was a bird of passage, that the frozen Arctic could be no more than a whim to her. They deferred a little to her because she knew the great world—New York, Vienna, London, Paris. Great names fell from her lips casually and carelessly. She referred familiarly to princes and famous statesmen, as if she had gossiped with them tête-à-tête over the teacups. She was full of spicy little anecdotes about German royalty and the British aristocracy. It was no wonder, Gordon Elliot thought, that she had rather stunned the little social set of Kusiak.

Through Northrup and Trelawney a new slant

on Macdonald was given to Gordon. He had fallen into casual talk with them after dinner on the fore deck. It was still raining, but all three were equipped with slickers or mackintoshes. To his surprise the young man discovered that they bore him no grudge at all for his interference the night before.

"But we ain't through with Colby Macdonald yet," Trelawney explained. "Mind, I don't say we're going to get him. Nothing like that. He knocked me cold with that loaded suitcase of his. By the looks of him I'm even for that. Good enough. But here's the point. We stand for Labor. He stands for Capital. See? Things ain't what they used to be in Alaska, and it's because of Colby Macdonald and his friends. They're grabbers—that's what they are. They want the whole works. A hell of a roar goes up from them when the Government stops their combines, but all the time they're bearing down a little harder on us workingmen. Understand? It's up to us to fight, ain't it?"

Later Elliot put this viewpoint before Strong.

"There's something in it," the miner agreed. "Wages have gone down, and it's partly because the big fellows are consolidating interests. Alaska ain't a poor man's country the way it was. But Mac ain't to blame for that. He has to play the game the way the cards are dealt out."

The sky was clear again when the Hannah drew

in to the wharf at Moose Head to unload freight, but the mud in the unpaved street leading to the business section of the little frontier town was instep deep. Many of the passengers hurried ashore to make the most of the five-hour stop. Macdonald, with Mrs. Mallory and their Kusiak friends, disappeared in a bus. Elliot put on a pair of heavy boots and started uptown.

At the end of the wharf he passed Miss O'Neill. She wore no rubbers and she had come to a halt at the beginning of the mud. After a momentary indecision she returned slowly to the boat.

The young man walked up into the town, but ten minutes later he crossed the gangplank of the Hannah again with a package under his arm. Miss O'Neill was sitting on the forward deck making a pretense to herself of reading. This was where Elliot had expected to find her, but now that the moment of attack had come he had to take his fear by the throat. When he had thought of it first there seemed nothing difficult about offering to do her a kindness, yet he found himself shrinking from the chance of a rebuff.

He moved over to where she sat and lifted his hat. "I hope you won't think it a liberty, Miss O'Neill, but I've brought you some rubbers from a store uptown. I noticed you couldn't get ashore without them."

Gordon tore the paper wrapping from his package and disclosed half a dozen pairs of rubbers.

The girl was visibly embarrassed. She was not at all certain of the right thing to do. Where she had been brought up young men did not offer courtesies of this sort so informally.

"I—I think I won't need them, thank you. I've decided not to leave the boat," she answered shyly.

Elliot had never been accused of being a quitter. Having begun this, he proposed to see it out. He caught sight of the purser superintending the discharge of cargo and called to him by name. The officer joined them, a pad of paper and a pencil in his hand.

"I'm trying to persuade Miss O'Neill that she ought to go ashore while we're lying here. What was it you told me about the waterfall back of the town?"

"Finest thing of its kind in Alaska. They're so proud of it in this burg that they would like to make it against the law for any one to leave without seeing it. Every one takes it in. We won't get away till night. You've plenty of time if you want to see it."

"Now, will you please introduce me to Miss O'Neill formally?"

The purser went through the usual formula of presentation, adding that Elliot was a government official on his way to Kusiak. Having done his duty by the young man, the busy supercargo retired.

"I'm sure it would do you good to walk up to the waterfall with me, Miss O'Neill," urged Elliot.

She met a little dubiously the smile that would not stay quite extinguished on his good-looking, boyish face. Why shouldn't she go with him, since it was the American way for unchaperoned youth to enjoy itself naturally?

"If they'll fit," the girl answered, eyeing the rubbers.

Gordon dropped to his knee and demonstrated that they would.

As they walked along the muddy street she gave him a friendly little nod of thanks. "Good of you to take the trouble to look out for me."

He laughed. "It was myself I was looking out for. I'm a stranger in the country and was awfully lonesome."

"Is it that this is your first time in too?" she asked shyly.

"You're going to Kusiak, aren't you? Do you know anybody there?" replied Elliot.

"My cousin lives there, but I haven't seen her since I was ten. She's an American. Eleven years ago she visited us in Ireland."

"I'm glad you know some one," he said. "You'll not be so lonesome with some of your people living there. I have two friends at Kusiak—a girl I used to go to school with and her husband."

"Are you going to live at Kusiak?"

43

"No; but I'll be stationed in the Territory for several months. I'll be in and out of the town a good deal. I hope you'll let me see something of you."

The fine Irish coloring deepened in her cheeks. He had a way of taking in his stride the barriers between them, but it was impossible for her to feel offended at this cheery, vigorous young fellow with the winning smile and the firm-set jaw. She liked the warmth in his honest brown eyes. She liked the play of muscular grace beneath his well-fitting clothes. The sinuous ease of his lean, wide-shouldered body stirred faintly some primitive instinct in her maiden heart. Sheba did not know, as her resilient muscles carried her forward joyfully, that she was answering the call of youth to youth.

Gordon respected her shyness and moved warily to establish his contact. He let the talk drift to impersonal topics as they picked their way out from the town along the mossy trail. The ground was spongy with water. On either side of them ferns and brakes grew lush. Sheba took the porous path with a step elastic. To the young man following she seemed a miracle of supple lightness.

The trail tilted up from the lowlands, led across dips, and into a draw. A little stream meandered down and gurgled over rocks worn smooth by ages of attrition. Alders brushed the stream and their foliage checkered the trail with sunlight and shadow.

They were ascending steadily now along a pathway almost too indistinct to follow. The air was aromatic with pine from a grove that came straggling down the side of a gulch to the brook.

"Do you know, I have a queer feeling that I've seen all this before," the Irish girl said. "Of course I haven't—unless it was in my dreams. Naturally I've thought about Alaska a great deal because my father lived here."

"I didn't know that."

"Yes. He came in with the Klondike stampeders." She added quietly: "He died on Bonanza Creek two years later."

"Was he a miner?"

"Not until he came North. He had an interest in a claim. It later turned out worthless."

A bit of stiff climbing brought them to a boulder field back of which rose a mountain ridge.

"We've got off the trail somehow," Elliot said. "But I don't suppose it matters. If we keep going we're bound to come to the waterfall."

Beyond the boulder field the ridge rose sharply. Gordon looked a little dubiously at Sheba.

"Are you a good climber?"

As she stood in the sunpour, her cheeks flushed with exercise, he could see that her spirit courted adventure.

"I'm sure I must be," she answered with a smile

adorable. "I believe I could do the Matterhorn to-day."

Well up on the shoulder of the ridge they stopped to breathe. The distant noise of falling water came faintly to them.

"We're too far to the left—must have followed the wrong spur," Elliot explained. " Probably we can cut across the face of the mountain."

Presently they came to an impasse. The gulch between the two spurs terminated in a rock wall that fell almost sheer for two hundred feet.

The color in the cheeks beneath the eager eyes of the girl was warm. "Let's try it," she begged.

The young man had noticed that she was as sure-footed as a mountain goat and that she could stand on the edge of a precipice without dizziness. The surface of the wall was broken. What it might be beyond he could not tell, but the first fifty feet was a bit of attractive and not too difficult rock traverse.

Now and again he made a suggestion to the young woman following him, but for the most part he trusted her to choose her own foot and hand holds. Her delicacy was silken strong. If she was slender, she was yet deep-bosomed. The movements of the girl were as certain as those of an experienced mountaineer.

The way grew more difficult. They had been following a ledge that narrowed till it ran out. Jutting knobs of feldspar and stunted shrubs growing from crevices offered toe-grips instead of the even foothold of the rock shelf. As Gordon looked down at the dizzy fall beneath them his judgment told him they had better go back. He said as much to his companion.

The smile she flashed at him was delightfully provocative. It served to point the figure she borrowed from Gwen. "So you think I'm a 'fraid-cat, Mr. Elliot?"

His inclination marched with hers. It was their first adventure together and he did not want to spoil it by undue caution. There really was not much danger yet so long as they were careful.

Gordon abandoned the traverse and followed an ascending crack in the wall. The going was hard. It called for endurance and muscle, as well as for a steady head and a sure foot. He looked down at the girl wedged between the slopes of the granite trough.

She read his thought. "The old guard never surrenders, sir," was her quick answer as she brushed in salute with the tips of her fingers a stray lock of hair.

The trough was worse than Elliot had expected. It had in it a good deal of loose rubble that started in small slides at the least pressure.

"Be very careful of your footing," he called back anxiously.

A small grassy platform lay above the upper end of the trough, but the last dozen feet of the approach was a very difficult bit. Gordon took advantage of every least projection. He fought his way up with his back against one wall and his knees pressed to the other. Three feet short of the platform the rock walls became absolutely smooth. The climber could reach within a foot of the top.

"Are you stopped?" asked Sheba.

"Looks that way."

A small pine projected from the edge of the shelf out over the precipice. It might be strong enough to bear his weight. It might not. Gordon unbuckled his belt and threw one end over the trunk of the dwarf tree. Gingerly he tested it with his weight, then went up hand over hand and worked himself over the edge of the little plateau.

"All right?" the girl called up.

"All right. But you can't make it. I'm coming down again."

"I'm going to try."

"I wouldn't, Miss O'Neill. It's really dangerous."

"I'd like to try it. I'll stop if it's too hard," she promised.

The strength of her slender wrists surprised him. She struggled up the vertical crevasse inch by inch. His heart was full of fear, for a misstep now would be fatal. He lay down with his face over the ledge and lowered to her the buckled loop of his belt. Twice she stopped exhausted, her back and her hands pressed against the walls of the trough angle for support.

"Better give it up," he advised.

"I'll not then." She smiled stubbornly as she shook her head.

Presently her fingers touched the belt.

Gordon edged forward an inch or two farther. "Put your hand through the loop and catch hold of the leather above," he told her.

She did so, and at the same instant her foot slipped. The girl swung out into space suspended by one wrist. The muscles of Elliot hardened into steel as they responded to the strain. His body began to slide very slowly down the incline.

In a moment the acute danger was past. Sheba had found a hold with her feet and relieved somewhat the dead pull upon Elliot.

She had not voiced a cry, but the face that looked up into his was very white.

"Take your time," he said in a quiet, matter-of-fact way.

With his help she came close enough for him to reach her hand. After that it was only a moment before she knelt on the plateau beside him.

"Touch and go, wasn't it?" Sheba tried to smile, but the colorless lips told the young man she was still faint from the shock.

He knew he was going to reproach himself bitterly for having led her into such a risk, but he could not just now afford to waste his energies on regrets. Nor could he let her mind dwell on past dangers so long as there were future ones to be faced.

"You might have sprained your wrist," he said lightly as he rose to examine the cliff still to be negotiated.

Her dark eyes looked at him with quick surprise. "So I might," she answered dryly.

But his indifferent tone had the effect upon her of a plunge into cold water. It braced and stiffened her will. If he wanted to ignore the terrible danger through which she had passed, certainly she was not going to remind him of it.

Between where they stood and the summit of the cliff was another rock traverse. A kind of rough, natural stairway led down to a point opposite them. But before this could be reached thirty feet of granite must be crossed. The wall looked hazardous enough in all faith. It lay in the shade, and there were spots where a thin coating of ice covered the smooth slabs. But there was no other way up, and if the traverse could be made the rest was easy.

Gordon was mountaineer enough to know that the climb up is safer than the one back. The only possible way for them to go down the trough was for him to lower her by the belt until she found footing enough to go alone. He did not quite admit it to himself, but in his heart he doubted whether she could make it safely.

The alternative was the cliff face.

CHAPTER V
ACROSS THE TRAVERSE

Elliot took off his shoes and turned toward the traverse.

"Think I'll see if I can cross to that stairway. You had better wait here, Miss O'Neill, until we find out if it can be done."

His manner was casual, his voice studiously light.

Sheba looked across the cliff and down to the boulder bed two hundred feet below. "You can never do it in the world. Isn't there another way up?"

"No. The wall above us slopes out. I've got to cross to the stairway. If I make it I'm going to get a rope."

"Do you mean you're going back to town for one?"

"Yes."

Her eyes fastened to his in a long, unspoken question. She read the answer. He was afraid to have her try the trough again. To get back to town by way of their roundabout ascent would waste time. If he was going to rescue her before night, he must take the shortest cut, and that was across the face of the sheer cliff. For the first time

51

she understood how serious was their plight.

"We can go back together by the trough, can't we?" But even as she asked, her heart sank at the thought of facing again that dizzy height. The moment of horror when she had thought herself lost had shaken her nerve.

"It would be difficult."

The glance of the girl swept again the face of the wall he must cross. It could not be done without a rope. Her fear-filled eyes came back to his.

"It's my fault. I made you come," she said in a low voice.

"Nonsense," he answered cheerfully. "There's no harm done. If I can't reach the stairway I can come back and go down by the trough."

Sheba assented doubtfully.

It had come on to drizzle again. The rain was fine and cold, almost a mist, and already it was forming a film of ice on the rocks.

"I can't take time to go back by the trough. The point is that I don't want you camped up here after night. There has been no sun on this side of the spur and in the chill of the evening it must get cold even in summer."

He was making his preparations as he talked. His coat he took off and threw down. His shoes he tied by the laces to his belt.

"I'll try not to be very long," he promised.

"It's God's will then, so it is," she sighed, relapsing into the vernacular.

Her voice was low and not very steady, for the heart of the girl was heavy. She knew she must not protest his decision. That was not the way to play the game. But somehow the salt had gone from their light-hearted adventure. She had become panicky from the moment when her feet had started the rubble in the trough and gone flying into the air. The gayety that had been the note of their tramp had given place to fears.

Elliot took her little hand in a warm, strong grip. "You're not going to be afraid. We'll work out all right, you know."

"Yes."

"It's not just the thing to leave a lady in the rain when you take her for a walk, but it can't be helped. We'll laugh about it to-morrow."

Would they? she wondered, answering his smile faintly. Her courage was sapped. She wanted to cry out that he must not try the traverse, but she set her will not to make it harder for him.

He turned to the climb.

"You've forgotten your coat," she reminded.

"I'm traveling light this trip. You'd better slip it on before you get chilled."

Sheba knew he had left it on purpose for her.

Her fascinated eyes followed him while he moved out from the plateau across the face of the precipice. His hand had found a knob of projecting feldspar and he was feeling with his right foot for a hold in some moss that grew in a crevice. He had none of the tools for climbing—no rope, no hatchet, none of the support of numbers. All the allies he could summon were his bare hands and feet, his resilient muscles, and his stout heart. To make it worse, the ice film from the rain coated every jutting inch of quartz with danger.

But he worked steadily forward, moving with the infinite caution of one who knows that there will be no chance to remedy later any mistake. A slight error in judgment, the failure in response of any one of fifty muscles, would send him plunging down.

Occasionally he spoke to Sheba, but she volunteered no remarks. It was her part to wait and watch while he concentrated every faculty upon his task. He had come to an impasse after crossing a dozen feet of the wall and was working up to get around a slab of granite which protruded, a convex barrier, from the surface of the cliff. It struck the girl that from a distance he must look like a fly on a pane of glass. Even to her, close as she was, that smooth rock surface looked impossible.

Her eye left him for an instant to sweep the gulf below. She gave a little cry, ran to his coat, and began to wave it. For the first time since Elliot had begun the traverse she took the initiative in speech.

"I see some people away over to the left, Mr.

Elliot. I'm going to call to them." Her voice throbbed with hope.

But it was not her shouts or his, which would not have carried one tenth the distance, that reached the group in the valley. One of them caught a glimpse of the wildly waving coat. There was a consultation and two or three fluttered handkerchiefs in response. Presently they moved on.

Sheba could not believe her eyes. "They're not leaving us surely?" she gasped.

"That's what they're doing," answered Gordon grimly. "They think we're calling to them out of vanity to show them where we climbed."

"Oh!" She strangled a sob in her throat. Her heart was weighted as with lead.

"I'm going to make it. I think I see my way from here," her companion called across to her. "A fault runs to the foot of the stairway, if I can only do the next yard or two."

He did them, by throwing caution to the winds. An icy, rounded boulder projected above him out of reach. He unfastened his belt again and put the shoes, tied by the laces, around his neck. There was one way to get across to the ledge of the fault. He took hold of the two ends of the belt, crouched, and leaned forward on tiptoes toward the knob. The loop of the belt slid over the ice-coated boss. There was no chance to draw back now, to test the hold he had gained. If the leather slipped he was lost. His body swung across the abyss and his feet landed on the little ledge beyond.

His shout of success came perhaps ten minutes later. "I've reached the stairway, Miss O'Neill. I'll try not to be long, but you'd better exercise to keep up the circulation. Don't worry, please. I'll be back before night."

"I'm so glad," she cried joyfully. "I was afraid for you. And I'll not worry a bit. Good-bye."

Elliot made his way up to the summit and ran along a footpath which brought him to a bridge across the mountain stream just above the falls. The trail zigzagged down the turbulent little river close to the bank. Before he had specialized on the short distances Gordon had been a cross-country runner. He was in fair condition and he covered the ground fast.

About a mile below the falls he met two men. One of them was Colby Macdonald. He carried a coil of rope over one shoulder. The big Alaskan explained that he had not been able to get it out of his head that perhaps the climbers who had waved at his party had been in difficulties. So he had got a rope from the cabin of an old miner and was on his way back to the falls.

The three climbed to the falls, crossed the bridge, and reached the top of the cliff.

"You know the lay of the land down there, Mr. Elliot. We'll lower you," decided Macdonald, who took command as a matter of course.

Gordon presently stood beside Sheba on the little plateau. She had quite recovered from the touch of hysteria that had attacked her courage. The wind and the rain had whipped the color into her soft cheeks, had disarranged a little the crinkly, blue-black hair, wet tendrils of which nestled against her temples. The health and buoyancy of the girl were in the live eyes that met his eagerly.

"You weren't long," was all she said.

"I met them coming," he answered as he dropped the loop of the rope over her head and arranged it under her shoulders.

He showed her how to relieve part of the strain of the rope on her flesh by using her hands to lift.

"All ready?" Macdonald called from above.

"All ready," Elliot answered. To Sheba he said, "Hold tight."

The girl was swung from the ledge and rose jerkily in the air. She laughed gayly down at her friend below.

"It's fun."

Gordon followed her a couple of minutes later. She was waiting to give him a hand over the edge of the cliff.

"Miss O'Neill, this is Mr. Macdonald," he said, as soon as he had freed himself from the rope. "You are fellow passengers on the Hannah."

Macdonald was looking at her straight and hard.

"Your father's name—was it Farrell O'Neill?" he asked bluntly.

"Yes."

"I knew him."

The girl's eyes lit. "I'm glad, Mr. Macdonald. That's one reason I wanted to come to Alaska—to hear about my father's life here. Will you tell me?"

"Sometime. We must be going now to catch the boat—after I've had a look at the cliff this young man crawled across."

He turned away, abruptly it struck Elliot, and climbed down the natural stairway up which the young man had come. Presently he rejoined those above. Macdonald looked at Elliot with a new respect.

"You're in luck, my friend, that we're not carrying you from the foot of the cliff," he said dryly. "I wouldn't cross that rock wall for a hundred thousand dollars in cold cash."

"Nor I again," admitted Gordon with a laugh. "But we had either to homestead that plateau or vacate it. I preferred the latter."

Miss O'Neill's deep eyes looked at him. She was about to speak, then changed her mind.

CHAPTER VI
SHEBA SINGS—
AND TWO MEN LISTEN

Elliot did not see Miss O'Neill next morning until she appeared in the dining-room for breakfast. He timed himself to get through so as to join her when she left. They strolled out to the deck together.

"Did you sleep well?" he asked.

"After I fell asleep. It took me a long time. I kept seeing you on the traverse."

He came abruptly to what was on his mind. "I have an apology to make, Miss O'Neill. If I made light of your danger yesterday, it was because I was afraid you might break down. I had to seem unsympathetic rather than risk that."

She smiled forgiveness. "All you said was that I might have sprained my wrist. It was true too. I might have—and I did." Sheba showed a white linen bandage tied tightly around her wrist.

"Does it pain much?"

"Not so much now. It throbbed a good deal last night."

"Your whole weight came on it with a wrench. No wonder it hurt."

Sheba noticed that the Hannah was drawing

up to a wharf and the passengers were lining up with their belongings. "Is this where we change?"

"Those of us going to Kusiak transfer here. But there's no hurry. We wait at this landing two hours."

Gordon helped Sheba move her baggage to the other boat and joined her on deck. They were both strangers in the land. Their only common acquaintance was Macdonald and he was letting Mrs. Mallory absorb his attention just now. Left to their own resources the two young people naturally drifted together a good deal.

This suited Elliot. He found his companion wholly delightful, not the less because she was so different from the girls he knew at home. She could be frank, and even shyly audacious on occasion, but she held a little note of reserve he felt bound to respect. Her experience of the world had clearly been limited. She was not at all sure of herself, of the proper degree of intimacy to permit herself with a strange and likable young man who had done her so signal a service.

Macdonald left the boat twenty miles below Kusiak with Mrs. Mallory and the Selfridges. A chauffeur with a motor-car was waiting on the wharf to run them to town, but he gave the wheel to Macdonald and took the seat beside the driver.

The little miner Strong grinned across to Elliot, who was standing beside Miss O'Neill at the boat rail.

"That's Mac all over. He hires a fellow to run his car—brings him up here from Seattle—and then takes the wheel himself every time he rides. I don't somehow see Mac sitting back and letting another man run the machine."

It was close to noon before the river boat turned a bend and steamed up to the wharf at Kusiak. The place was an undistinguished little log town that rambled back from the river up the hill in a hit-or-miss fashion. Its main street ran a tortuous course parallel to the stream.

Half of the town, it seemed, was down to meet the boat.

"Are you going to the hotel or direct to your cousin's?" Gordon asked Miss O'Neill.

"To my cousin's. I fancy she's down here to meet me. It was arranged that I come on this boat."

There was much waving of handkerchiefs and shouting back and forth as the steamer slowly drew close to the landing.

Elliot caught a glimpse of the only people in Kusiak he had known before coming in, but though he waved to them he saw they did not recognize him. After the usual delay about getting ashore he walked down the gangway carrying the suitcases of the Irish girl. Sheba followed at his heels. On the wharf he came face to face with a slender, well-dressed young woman.

"Diane!" he cried.

She stared at him. "You! What in Heaven's

61

name are you doing here, Gordon Elliot?" she demanded, and before he could answer had seized both hands and turned excitedly to call a stocky man near. "Peter—Peter! Guess who's here?"

"Hello, Paget!" grinned Gordon, and he shook hands with the husband of Diane.

Elliot turned to introduce his friend, but she anticipated him.

"Cousin Diane," she said shyly. "Don't you know me?"

Mrs. Paget swooped down upon the girl and smothered her in her embrace.

"This is Sheba—little Sheba that I have told you so often about, Peter," she cried. "Glory be, I'm glad to see you, child." And Diane kissed her again warmly. "You two met on the boat, of course, coming in. I hope you didn't let her get lonesome, Gordon. Look after Sheba's suitcases, Peter. You'll come to dinner to-night, Gordon— at seven."

"I'm in the kind hands of my countrywoman," laughed Gordon. "I'll certainly be on hand."

"But what in the world are you doing here? You're the last man I'd have expected to see."

"I'm in the service of the Government, and I've been sent in on business."

"Well, I'm going to say something original, dear people," Mrs. Paget replied. "It's a small world, isn't it?"

While he was dressing for dinner later in the day, Elliot recalled early memories of the Pagets. He had known Diane ever since they had been youngsters together at school. He remembered her as a restless, wiry little thing, keen as a knife-blade. She had developed into a very pretty girl, alive, ambitious, energetic, with a shrewd eye to the main chance. Always popular socially, she had surprised everybody by refusing the catch of the town to marry a young mining engineer without a penny. Gordon was in college at the time, but during the next long vacation he had fraternized a good deal with the Peter Pagets. The young married people had been very much in love with each other, but not too preoccupied to take the college boy into their happiness as a comrade. Diane always had been a manager, and she liked playing older sister to so nice a lad. He had been on a footing friendly enough to drop in unannounced whenever he took the fancy. If they were out, or about to go out, the freedom of the den, a magazine, and good tobacco had been his. Then the Arctic gold-fields had claimed Paget and his bride. That had been more than ten years ago, and until to-day Gordon had not seen them since.

While Elliot was brushing his dinner coat before the open window of the room assigned him at the hotel, somebody came out to the porch below. The voice of a woman floated faintly to him.

"Seen Diane's Irish beauty yet, Ned?"

"Yes," a man answered.

The woman laughed softly. "Mrs. Mallory came up on the same boat with her." The inflection suggested that the words were meant not to tell a fact, but some less obvious inference.

"Oh, you women!" the man commented good-naturedly.

"She's wonderfully pretty, and of course Diane will make the most of her. But Mrs. Mallory is a woman among ten thousand."

"I'd choose the girl if it were me," said the man.

"But it isn't you. We'll see what we'll see."

They were moving up the street and Gordon heard no more. What he had heard was not clear to him. Why should any importance attach to the fact that Mrs. Mallory and Sheba O'Neill had come up the river on the same boat? Yet he was vaguely disturbed by the insinuation that in some way Diane was entering her cousin as a rival of the older woman. He resented the idea that the fine, young personality of the Irish girl was being cheapened by management on the part of Diane Paget.

Elliot was not the only dinner guest at the Paget home that evening. He found Colby Macdonald sitting in the living-room with Sheba. She came quickly forward to meet the newly arrived guest.

"Mr. Macdonald has been telling me about my

father. He knew him on Frenchman Creek where they both worked claims," explained the girl.

The big mining man made no comment and added nothing to what she said. There were times when his face was about as expressive as a stone wall. Except for a hard wariness in the eyes it told nothing now.

The dinner went off very well. Diane and Peter had a great many questions to ask Gordon about old friends. By the time these had been answered Macdonald was chatting easily with Sheba. The man had been in many out-of-the-way corners of the world, had taken part in much that was dramatic and interesting. If the experience of the Irish girl had been small, her imagination had none the less gone questing beyond the narrow bars of her life upon amazing adventure. She listened with glowing eyes to the strange tales this man of magnificent horizons had to tell. Never before had she come into contact with any one like him.

The others too succumbed to his charm. He dominated that little dining-room because he was a sixty-horse-power dynamo. For all his bulk he was as lean as a panther and as sinewy. There was virility in the very economy of his motions, in the reticence of his speech. Not even a fool could have read weakness there. When he followed Sheba into the living-room, power trod in his long, easy stride.

Paget was superintendent of the Lucky Strike, a mine owned principally by Macdonald. The two talked business for a few minutes over their cigars, but Diane interrupted gayly to bring them back into the circle. Adroitly she started Macdonald on the account of a rescue of two men lost in a blizzard the year before. He had the gift of dramatizing his story, of selecting only effective details. There was no suggestion of boasting. If he happened to be the hero of any of his stories the fact was of no importance to him. It was merely a detail of the picture he was sketching.

Gordon interrupted with a question a story he was telling of a fight he had seen between two bull moose.

"Did you say that was while you were on the way over to inspect the Kamatlah coal-fields for the first time?"

The eyes of the young man were quick with interest.

"Yes."

"Four years ago last spring?"

Macdonald looked at him with a wary steadiness. Some doubt had found lodgment in his mind. Before he could voice it, if, indeed, he had any such intention, Elliot broke in swiftly,—

"Don't answer that question. I asked it without proper thought. I am a special agent of the General Land Office sent up to investigate the

Macdonald coal claims and kindred interests."

Slowly the rigor of the big Scotchman's steely eyes relaxed to a smile that was genial and disarming. If this news hit him hard he gave no sign of it. And that it was an unexpected blow there could be no doubt.

"Glad you've come, Mr. Elliot. We ask nothing but fair play. Tell the truth, and we'll thank you. The men who own the Macdonald group of claims have nothing to conceal. I'll answer that question. I meant to say two years ago last spring."

His voice was easy and his gaze unwavering as he made the correction, yet everybody in the room except Sheba knew he was deliberately lying to cover the slip. For the admission that he had inspected the Kamatlah field just before his dummies had filed upon it would at least tend to aggravate suspicion that the entries were not *bona-fide*.

It was rather an awkward moment. Diane blamed herself because she had brought the men together socially. Why had she not asked Gordon more explicitly what his business was? Peter grinned a little uncomfortably. It was Sheba who quite unconsciously relieved the situation.

"But what about the big moose, Mr. Macdonald? What did it do then?"

The Alaskan went back to his story. He was talking for Sheba alone, for the young girl with eager, fascinated eyes which flashed with sympathy as they devoured selected glimpses of his wild, turbulent career. Her clean, brave spirit was throwing a glamour over the man. She saw him with other eyes than Elliot's. The Government official admired him tremendously. Macdonald was an empire-builder. He blazed trails for others to follow in safety. But Gordon could guess how callously his path was strewn with brutality, with the effects of an ethical color-blindness largely selfish, though even he did not know that the man's primitive jungle code of wolf eat wolf had played havoc with Sheba's young life many years before.

Diane, satisfied that Macdonald had scored, called upon Sheba.

"I want you to sing for us, dear, if you will."

Sheba accompanied herself. The voice of the girl had no unusual range, but it was singularly sweet and full of the poignant feeling that expresses the haunting pathos of her race.

> "It's well I know ye, Shevè Cross,
>   ye weary, stony hill,
> An' I'm tired, och, I'm tired to be
>   looking on ye still.
> For here I live the near side
>   an' he is on the far,
> An' all your heights and hollows are
>   between us, so they are.
>   Och anee!"

Gordon, as he listened, felt the strange hunger of that homesick cry steal through his blood. He saw his own emotions reflected in the face of the Scotch-Canadian, who was watching with a tense interest the slim, young figure at the piano, the girl whose eyes were soft and dewy with the mysticism of her people, were still luminous with the poetry of the child in spite of the years that heralded her a woman.

Elliot intercepted the triumphant sweep of Diane's glance from Macdonald to her husband. In a flash it lit up for him the words he had heard on the hotel porch. Diane, an inveterate matchmaker, intended her cousin to marry Colby Macdonald. No doubt she thought she was doing a fine thing for the girl. He was a millionaire, the biggest figure in the Northwest. His iron will ran the town and district as though the people were chattels of his. Back of him were some of the biggest financial interests in the United States.

But the gorge of Elliot rose. The man, after all, was a law-breaker, a menace to civilization. He was a survivor by reason of his strength from the primitive wolf-pack. Already the special agent had heard many strange stories of how this man of steel had risen to supremacy by trampling down lesser men with whom he had had dealings, of terrible battles from which his lean, powerful body had emerged bloody and battered, but victorious. The very look of his hard, gray eyes was dominant and masterful. He would win, no matter how. It came to Gordon's rebel heart that if Macdonald wanted this lovely Irish girl,—and the young man never doubted that the Scotchman would want her,—he would reach out and gather in Sheba just as if she were a coal mine or a placer prospect.

All this surged through the mind of the young man while the singer was on the first line of the second stanza.

"But if 't was only Shevè Cross
    to climb from foot to crown,
I'd soon be up an' over that,
    I'd soon be runnin' down.
Then sure the great ould sea itself
    is there beyont the bar,
An' all the windy wathers are
    between us, so they are.
                Och anee!"

The rich, soft, young voice with its Irish brogue died away. The little audience paid the singer the tribute of silence. She herself was the first to speak.

"'Divided' is the name of it. A namesake of mine, Moira O'Neill, wrote it," she explained.

"It's a beautiful song, and I thank ye for singing it," Macdonald said simply. "It minds me of my own barefoot days by the Tay."

Later in the evening the two dinner guests walked back to the hotel together. The two subjects uppermost in the minds of both were not mentioned by either. They discussed casually the cost of living in the North, the raising of strawberries at Kusiak, and the best way to treat the mosquito nuisance, but neither of them referred to the Macdonald coal claims or to Sheba O'Neill.

CHAPTER VII
WALLY GETS ORDERS

Macdonald, from his desk, looked up at the man in the doorway. Selfridge had come in jauntily, a cigar in his mouth, but at sight of the grim face of his chief the grin fled.

"Come in and shut the door," ordered the Scotchman. "I sent for you to congratulate you, Wally. You did fine work outside. You told me, didn't you, that it was all settled at last—that our claims are clear-listed for patent?"

The tubby little man felt the edge of irony in the quiet voice. "Sure. That's what Winton told me," he assented nervously.

"Then you'll be interested to know that a special field agent of the Land Department sat opposite me last night and without batting an eye came across with the glad news that he was here to investigate our claims."

Selfridge bounced up like a rubber ball from the chair into which he had just settled. "What!"

"Pleasant surprise, isn't it? I've been wondering what you were doing outside. Of course I know you had to take in the shows and cabarets of New York. But couldn't you edge in an hour or two once a week to attend to business?"

73

Wally's collar began to choke him. The cool, hard words of the big Scotchman pelted like hail.

"Must be a bluff, Mac. The muckrake magazines have raised such a row about the Guttenchild crowd putting over a big steal on the public that the party leaders are scared stiff. I couldn't pick up a newspaper anywhere without seeing your name in the headlines. It was fierce." Selfridge had found his glib tongue and was off.

"I understand that, Wally. What I don't get is how you came to let them slip this over on you without even a guess that it was going to happen."

That phase of the subject Selfridge did not want to discuss.

"Bet you a hat I've guessed it right—just a grand-stand play of the Administration to fool the dear people. This fellow has got his orders to give us a clean bill of health. Sure. That must be it. I suppose it's this man Elliot that came up on the boat with us."

"Yes."

"Well, that's easy. If he hasn't been seen we can see him."

Macdonald looked his man Friday over with a scarcely veiled contempt. "You have a beautiful, childlike faith in every man's dishonesty, Wally. Did it ever occur to you that some people are straight—that they won't sell out?"

"All he gets is a beggarly two thousand or so a year. We can fix him all right."

"You've about as much vision as a breed trader. Unless I miss my guess Elliot isn't that kind. He'll go through to a finish. What I'd like to know is how his mind works. If he sees straight we're all right, but if he is a narrow conservation fanatic he might go ahead and queer the whole game."

"You wouldn't stand for that." The quick glance of Selfridge asked a question.

The lips of the Scotchman were like steel traps and his eyes points of steel. "We'll cross that bridge if we come to it. Our first move is to try to win him to see this thing our way. I'll have a casual talk with him before he leaves for Kamatlah and feel him out."

"What's he doing here at all? If he's investigating the Kamatlah claims, why does he go hundreds of miles out of his way to come in to Kusiak?" asked Selfridge.

Macdonald smiled sardonically. "He's doing this job right. Elliot as good as told me that he's on the job to look up my record thoroughly. So he comes to Kusiak first. In a few days he'll leave for Kamatlah. That's where you come in, Wally."

"How do you mean?"

"You're going to start for Kamatlah tomorrow. You'll arrange the stage before he gets there— see all the men and the foremen. Line them up

75

so they'll come through with the proper talk. If you have any doubts about whether you can trust some one, don't take any chances. Fire him out of the camp. Offer Elliot the company hospitality. Load him down with favors. Take him everywhere. Show him everything. But don't let him get any proofs that the claims are being worked under the same management."

"But he'll suspect it."

"You can't help his suspicions. Don't let him get proof. Cover all the tracks that show company control."

"I can fix that," he said. "But what about Holt? The old man won't do a thing but tell all he knows, and a lot more that he suspects. You know how bitter he is—and crazy. He ought to be locked away with the flitter-mice."

"You mustn't let Elliot meet Holt."

"How the deuce can I help it? No chance to keep them apart in that little hole. It can't be done."

"Can't it?"

Something in the quiet voice rang a bell of alarm in the timid heart of Selfridge.

"You mean—"

"A man who works for me as my lieutenant must have nerve, Wally. Have you got it? Will you take orders and go through with them?"

His hard eyes searched the face of the plump little man. This was a job he would have liked to do himself, but he could not get away just now. Selfridge was the only man about him he could trust with it.

Wally nodded. His lips were dry and parched. "Go to it. What am I to do?"

"Get Holt out of the way while Elliot is at Kamatlah."

"But, Good Lord, I can't keep the man tied up a month," protested the leading tenor of Kusiak.

"It isn't doing Holt any good to sit tight clamped to that claim of his. He needs a change. Besides, I want him away so that we can contest his claim. Run him up into the hills. Or send him across to Siberia on a whaler. Or, better still, have him arrested for insanity and send him to Nome. I'll get Judge Landor to hold him a while."

"That would give him an alibi for his absence and prevent a contest."

"That's right. It would."

"Leave it to me. The old man is going on a vacation, though he doesn't know it yet."

"Good enough, Wally. I'll trust you. But remember, this fight has reached an acute stage. No more mistakes. The devil of it is we never seem to land the knockout punch. We've beaten this bunch of reform idiots before Winton, before the Secretary of the Interior, before the President, and before Congress. Now they're beginning all over again. Where is it to end?"

"This is their last kick. Probably Guttenchild agreed to it so as to let the party go before the people at the next election without any apologies. Entirely formal investigation, I should say."

This might be true, or it might not. Macdonald knew that just now the American people, always impulsive in its thinking, was supporting strongly the movement for conservation. A searchlight had been turned upon the Kamatlah coal-fields. Magazines and newspapers had hammered it home to readers that the Guttenchild and allied interests were engaged in a big steal from the people of coal, timber, and power-site lands to the value of more than a hundred million dollars.

The trouble had originated in a department low, but it had spread until the Macdonald claims had become a party issue. The officials of the Land Office, as well as the National Administration, were friendly to the claimants. They had no desire to offend one of the two largest money groups in the country. But neither did they want to come to wreck on account of the Guttenchilds. They found it impossible to ignore the charge that the entries were fraudulent and if consummated would result in a wholesale robbery of the public domain. Superficial investigations had been made and the claimants whitewashed. But the clamor had persisted.

Though he denied it officially, Macdonald made a present to the public of the admission that the entries were irregular. Laws, he held, were made for men and should be interpreted to aid progress. Bad ones ought to be evaded.

The facts were simple enough. Macdonald was the original promoter of the Kamatlah coalfield. He had engaged dummy entrymen to take up one hundred and sixty acres each under the Homestead Act. Later he intended to consolidate the claims and turn them over to the Guttenchilds under an agreement by which he was to receive one eighth of the stock of the company formed to work the mines. The entries had been made, the fee accepted by the Land Office, and receipts issued. In course of time Macdonald had applied for patents.

Before these were issued the magazines began to pour in their broadsides, and since then the papers had been held up.

The conscience of Macdonald was quite clear. The pioneers in Alaska were building out of the Arctic waste a new empire for the United States, and he held that a fair Government could do no less than offer them liberal treatment. To lock up from present use vast resources needed by Alaskans would be a mistaken policy, a narrow and perverted application of the doctrine of conservation. The Territory should be thrown open to the world. If capital were invited in to do its share of the building, immigration would flow rapidly northward. Within the lives of the present generation the new empire would take shape and wealth would pour inevitably into the United States from its frozen treasure house.

The view held by Macdonald was one common to the whole Pacific Coast. Seattle, Portland, San Francisco were a unit in the belief that the Government had no right to close the door of Alaska and then put a padlock upon it.

Feminine voices drifted from the outer office. Macdonald opened the door to let in Mrs. Selfridge and Mrs. Mallory.

The latter lady, Paris-shod and gloved, shook hands smilingly with the Scotch-Canadian. "Of course we're intruders in business hours, though you'll tell us we're not," she suggested.

He was not a man to surrender easily to the spell of woman, but when he looked into her deep-lidded, smouldering eyes something sultry beat in his blood.

"Business may fly out of the window when Mrs. Mallory comes in at the door," he answered.

"How gallant of you, especially when I've come with an impertinent question." Her gay eyes mocked him as she spoke.

"Then I'll probably tell you to mind your own business," he laughed. "Let's have your question."

"I've just been reading the 'Transcontinental Magazine.' A writer there says that you are a highway robber and a gambler. I know you're a robber because all the magazines say so. But are you only a big gambler?"

He met her raillery without the least embarrassment.

"Sure I gamble. Every time I take a chance I'm gambling. So does everybody else. When you walk past the Flatiron Building you bet it won't fall down and crush you. We've got to take chances to live."

"How true, and I never thought of it," beamed Mrs. Selfridge. "What a philosopher you are, Mr. Macdonald."

The Scotchman went on without paying any attention to her effervescence. "I've gambled ever since I was a kid. I bet I could cross Death Valley and get out alive. That time I won. I bet it would rain once down in Arizona before my cattle died. I lost. Another time I took a contract to run a tunnel. In my bid I bet I wouldn't run into rock. My bank went broke that trip. When I joined the Klondike rush I was backing my luck to stand up. Same thing when I located the Kamatlah field. The coal might be a poor quality. Maybe I couldn't interest big capital in the proposition. Perhaps the Government would turn me down when I came to prove up. I was betting my last dollar against big odds. When I quit gambling it will be because I've quit living."

"And I suppose I'm a gambler too?" Mrs.

Mallory demanded with a little tilt of her handsome head.

He looked straight at her with the keen eyes that had bored through her from the first day they had met, the eyes that understood the manner of woman she was and liked her none the less.

"Of all the women I know you are the best gambler. It's born in you."

"Why, Mr. Macdonald!" screamed Mrs. Selfridge in her high staccato. "I don't think that's a compliment."

Mrs. Mallory did not often indulge in the luxury of a blush, but she changed color now. This big, blunt man sometimes had an uncanny divination. Did he, she asked herself, know what stake she was gambling for at Kusiak?

"You are too wise," she laughed with a touch of embarrassment very becoming. "But I suppose you are right. I like excitement."

"We all do. The only man who doesn't gamble is the convict in stripes, and the only reason he doesn't is that his chips are all gone. It's true that men on the frontier play for bigger stakes. They back their bets with all they have got and put their lives on top for good measure. But kids in the cradle all over the United States are going to live easier because of the gamblers at the dropping-off places. That writer fellow hit the nail on the head about me. My whole life is a gamble."

She moved with slow grace toward the door,

then over her shoulder flashed a sudden invitation at him. "Mrs. Selfridge and I are doing a little betting to-day, Big Chief Gambler. We're backing our luck that you two men will eat lunch with us at the Blue Bird Inn. Do we win?"

Macdonald reached for his hat promptly. "You win."

CHAPTER VIII
THE END OF THE PASSAGE

Wally Selfridge was a reliable business subordinate, even though he had slipped up in the matter of the appointment of Elliot. But when it came to facing the physical hardships of the North he was a malingerer. The Kamatlah trip had to be taken because his chief had ordered it, but the little man shirked the journey in his heart just as he knew his soft muscles would shrink from the aches of the trail.

His idea of work was a set of tennis on the outdoor wooden court of the Kusiak clubhouse, and even there his game was not a hard, smashing one, but an easy foursome with a girl for partner. He liked better to play bridge with attendants at hand to supply drinks and cigars. By nature he was a sybarite. The call of the frontier found no response in his sophisticated soul.

The part of the journey to be made by water was not so bad. Left to his own judgment, he would have gone to St. Michael's by boat and chartered a small steamer for the long trip along the coast through Bering Sea. But this would take time, and Macdonald did not mean to let him waste a day. He was to leave the river boat at the big bend and pack across country to Kamatlah. It would be a rough, heavy trail. The mosquitoes would be a continual torment. The cooking would be poor. And at the end of the long trek there awaited him monotonous months in a wretched coal camp far from all the comforts of civilization. No wonder he grumbled.

But though he grumbled at home and at the club and on the street about his coming exile, Selfridge made no complaints to Macdonald. That man of steel had no sympathy with the yearnings for the fleshpots. He was used to driving himself through discomfort to his end, and he expected as much of his deputies. Wherefore Wally took the boat at the time scheduled and waved a dismal farewell to wife and friends assembled upon the wharf.

Elliot said good-bye to the Pagets and Miss O'Neill ten days later. Diane was very frank with him.

"I hear you've been sleuthing around, Gordon, for facts about Colby Macdonald. I don't know what you have heard about him, but I hope you've got the sense to see how big a man he is and how much this country here owes him."

Gordon nodded agreement. "Yes, he's a big man."

"And he's good," added Sheba eagerly. "He never talks of it, but one finds out splendid things he has done."

The young man smiled, but not at all superciliously. He liked the stanch faith of the girl in her friend, even though his investigations had not led him to accept goodness as the outstanding quality of the Scotchman.

"I don't know what we would do without him," Diane went on. "Give him ten years and a free hand and Alaska will be fit for white people to live in. These attacks on him by newspapers and magazines are an outrage."

"It's plain that you are a partisan," charged Gordon gayly.

"I'm against locking up Alaska and throwing away the key, if that is what you mean by a partisan. We need this country opened up—the farms settled, the mines worked, the coal-fields developed, railroads built. It is one great big opportunity, the country here, and the narrow little conservation cranks want to shut it up tight from the people who have energy and foresight enough to help do the building."

"The Kusiak Chamber of Commerce ought to send you out as a lecturer to change public opinion, Diane. You are one enthusiastic little booster for freedom of opportunity," laughed the young man.

"Oh, well!" Diane joined in his laughter. It was one of her good points that she could laugh at herself. "I dare say I do sound like a real estate pamphlet, but it's all true anyhow."

Gordon left Kusiak as reluctantly as Wally

Selfridge had done, though his reasons for not wanting to go were quite different. They centered about a dusky-eyed young woman whom he had seen for the first time a fortnight before. He would have denied even to himself that he was in love, but whenever he was alone his thoughts reverted to Sheba O'Neill.

At the big bend Gordon left the river boat for his cross-country trek. Near the roadhouse was an Indian village where he had expected to get a guide for the journey to Kamatlah. But the fishing season had begun, and the men had all gone down river to take part in it.

The old Frenchman who kept the trading-post and roadhouse advised Gordon not to attempt the tramp alone.

"The trail it ees what you call dangerous. Feefty-Mile Swamp ees a monster that swallows men alive, Monsieur. You wait one week—two week—t'ree week, and some one will turn up to take you through," he urged.

"But I can't wait. And I have an official map of the trail. Why can't I follow it without a guide?" Elliot wanted to know impatiently.

The post-trader shrugged. "Maybeso, Monsieur—maybe not. Feefty-Mile—it ees one devil of a trail. No chechakoes are safe in there without a guide. I, Baptiste, know."

"Selfridge and his party went through a week ago. I can follow the tracks they left."

"But if it rains, Monsieur, the tracks will vaneesh, *n'est ce pas*? Lose the way, and the little singing folk will swarm in clouds about Monsieur while he stumbles through the swamp."

Elliot hesitated for the better part of a day, then came to an impulsive decision. He knew the evil fame of Fifty-Mile Swamp—that no trail in Alaska was held to be more difficult or dangerous. He knew too what a fearful pest the mosquitoes were. Peter had told him a story of how he and a party of engineers had come upon a man wandering in the hills, driven mad by mosquitoes. The traveler had lost his matches and had been unable to light smudge fires. Day and night the little singing devils had swarmed about him. He could not sleep. He could not rest. Every moment for forty-eight hours he had fought for his life against them. Within an hour of the time they found him the man had died a raving maniac.

But Elliot was well equipped with mosquito netting and with supplies. He had a reliable map, and anyhow he had only to follow the tracks left by the Selfridge party. He turned his back upon the big river and plunged into the wilderness.

There came a night when he looked up into the stars of the deep, still sky and knew that he was hundreds of miles from any other human being. Never in all his life had he been so much alone. He was not afraid, but there was something awesome in a world so empty of his kind. Sometimes he sang, and the sound of his voice at first startled him. It was like living in a world primeval, this traverse of a land so void of all the mechanism that man has built about him.

The tracks of the Selfridge party grew fainter after a night of rain. More rain fell, and they were obliterated altogether.

Gordon fished. He killed fresh game for his needs. Often he came on the tracks of moose and caribou. Sometimes, startled, they leaped into view quite close enough for a shot, but he used his rifle only to meet his wants. A huge grizzly faced him on the trail one afternoon, growled its menace, and went lumbering into the big rocks with awkward speed.

The way led through valley and morass, across hills and mountains. It wandered in a sort of haphazard fashion through a sun-bathed universe washed clean of sordidness and meanness. Always, as he pushed forward, the path grew more faint and uncertain. Elk runs crossed it here and there, so that often Gordon went astray and had to retrace his steps.

The maddening song of the mosquitoes was always with him. Only when he slept did he escape from it. The heavy gloves, the netting, the smudge fires were at best an insufficient protection.

It was the seventh night out that Elliot suspected he was off the trail. Rain sluiced down in torrents and next day continued to pour from a dun sky. His own tracks were blotted out and he searched for the trail in vain. Before the rain stopped, he was thoroughly disturbed in mind. It would be a serious business if he should be lost in the bad lands of the bogs. Even though he knew the general direction he must follow, there was no certainty that he would ever emerge from this swamp into which he had plunged.

Before he knew it he was entangled in Fifty-Mile. His map showed him the morass stretched for fifty miles to the south, but he knew that it had been charted hurriedly by a surveying party which had made no extensive explorations. A good deal of this country was *terra incognita*. It ran vaguely into a No Man's Land unknown to the prospector.

The going was heavy. Gordon had to pick his way through the mossy swamp, leading the pack-horse by the bridle. Sometimes he was ankle-deep in water of a greenish slime. Again he had to drag the animal from the bog to a hummock of grass which gave a spongy footing. This would end in another quagmire of peat through which they must plough with the mud sucking at their feet. It was hard, wearing toil. There was nothing to do but keep moving. The young man staggered forward till dusk. Utterly exhausted, he camped for the night on a hillock of moss that rose like an island in the swamp.

After he had eaten he fed his fire with green boughs that raised a dense smoke. He lay on the leeward side where the smoke drifted over him and fought mosquitoes till a shift of the wind lessened the plague. Toward midnight he rigged up a net for protection and crawled into his blankets. Instantly he fell sound asleep.

Elliot traveled next day by the compass. He had food for three days more, but he knew that no living man had the strength to travel for so long in such a morass. It was near midday when he lost his horse. The animal had bogged down several times and Gordon had wasted much time and spent a good deal of needed energy in dragging it to firmer footing. This time the pony refused to answer the whip. Its master unloaded pack and saddle. He tried coaxing; he tried the whip.

"Come, Old-Timer. One plunge, and you'll make it yet," he urged.

The pack-horse turned upon him dumb eyes of reproach, struggled to free its limbs from the mud, and sank down helplessly. It had traveled its last yard on the long Alaska trails.

After the sound of the shot had died away, Gordon struggled with the pack to the nearest hummock. He cut holes in a gunny-sack to fit his shoulders and packed into it his blankets, a saucepan, the beans, the coffee, and the diminished handful of flour. Into it went too the three slices of bacon that were left.

He hoisted the pack to his back and slipped his arms through the slits he had made. Painfully he labored forward over the quivering peat. Every weary muscle revolted at the demands his will imposed upon it. He drew on the last ounce of his strength and staggered forward. Sometimes he stumbled and went down into the oozing mud, minded to stay there and be done with the struggle. But the urge of life drove him to his feet again. It sent him pitching forward drunkenly. It carried him for weary miles after he despaired of ever covering another hundred yards.

With old, half-forgotten signals from the football field he spurred his will. Perhaps his mind was already beginning to wander, though through it all he held steadily to the direction that alone could save him.

He clapped his hands feebly and stooped for the plunge at the line of the enemy. " 'Attaboy, Gord—'attaboy—nine, eleven, seventeen. Hit 'er low, you Elliot."

When at last he went down to stay it was in an exhaustion so complete that not even his indomitable will could lash him to his feet again. For an hour he lay in a stupor, never stirring even to fight the swarm of mosquitoes that buzzed about him.

Toward evening he sat up and undid the pack from his back. The matches, in a tin box wrapped carefully with oilskin, were still perfectly dry. Soon he had a fire going and coffee boiling in the frying-pan. From the tin cup he carried strung on his belt he drank the coffee. It went through him like strong liquor. He warmed some beans and fried himself a slice of bacon, sopping up the grease with a cold biscuit left over from the day before.

Again he slept for a few hours. He had wound his watch mechanically and it showed him four o'clock when he took up the trail once more. In Seattle and San Francisco people were still asleep and darkness was heavy over the land. Here it had been day for a long time, ever since the summer sun, hidden for a while behind the low, distant hills, had come blazing forth again in a saddle between two peaks.

Gordon had reduced his pack by discarding a blanket, the frying-pan, and all the clothing he was not wearing. His rifle lay behind him in the swamp. He had cut to a minimum of safety what he was carrying, according to his judgment. But before long his last blanket was flung aside. He could not afford to carry an extra pound, for he knew he was running a race, the stakes of which were life and death.

A cloud of mosquitoes moved with him. He carried in his hand a spruce bough for defense against them. His hands were gloved, his face was covered with netting. But in spite of the best he could do they were an added torture.

Afternoon found him still staggering forward. The swamps were now behind him. He had won through at last by the narrowest margin possible. The ground was rising sharply toward the mountains. Across the range somewhere lay Kamatlah. But he was all in. With his food almost gone, a water supply uncertain, reserve strength exhausted, the chances of getting over the divide to safety were practically none.

He had come, so far as he could see, to the end of the passage.

CHAPTER IX
GID HOLT GOES PROSPECTING

As soon as Selfridge reached Kamatlah he began arranging the stage against the arrival of the Government agent. His preparations were elaborate and thorough. A young engineer named Howland had been in charge of the development work, but Wally rearranged his forces so as to let each dummy entryman handle the claim entered in his name. One or two men about whom he was doubtful he discharged and hurried out of the camp.

Selfridge had been given a free hand as to expenses and he oiled his way by liberal treatment of the men and by a judicious expenditure. He let them know pretty plainly that if the agent on his way to Kamatlah suspected corporate ownership of the claims, the Government would close down all work and there would be no jobs for them.

The company boarding-house became a restaurant, above which was suspended a newly painted sign with the legend, "San Francisco Grill, J. Glynn, Proprietor." The store also passed temporarily into the hands of its manager. Miners moved from the barracks that had been built by

Macdonald into hastily constructed cabins on the individual claims. Wally had always fancied himself as a stage manager for amateur theatricals. Now he justified his faith by transforming Kamatlah outwardly from a company camp to a mushroom one settled by wandering prospectors.

Gideon Holt alone was outside of all these activities and watched them with suspicion. He was an old-timer, sly but fearless, who hated Colby Macdonald with a bitter jealousy that could not be placated and he took no pains to hide the fact. He had happened to be in the vicinity prospecting when Macdonald had rushed his entries. Partly out of mere perversity and partly by reason of native shrewdness, old Holt had slipped in and located one of the best claims in the heart of the group. Nor had he been moved to a reasonable compromise by any amount of persuasion, threats, or tentative offers to buy a relinquishment. He was obstinate. He knew a good thing when he had it, and he meant to sit tight.

The adherents of the company might charge that Holt was cracked in the upper story, but none of them denied he was sharp as a street Arab. He guessed that all this preparation was not for nothing. Kamatlah was being dressed up to impress somebody who would shortly arrive. The first thought of Holt was that a group of big capitalists might be coming to look over their investment. But he rejected this surmise. There would be no need to try any deception upon them.

Mail from Seattle reached camp once a month. Holt sat down before his stove to read one of the newspapers he had brought from the office. It was the "P.-I." On the fifth page was a little boxed story that gave him his clue.

ELLIOT TO INVESTIGATE MACDONALD COAL CLAIMS

The reopening of the controversy as to the Macdonald claims, which had been clear-listed for patent by Harold B. Winton, the Commissioner of the General Land Office, takes on another phase with the appointment of Gordon Elliot as special field agent to examine the validity of the holdings. The new field agent won a reputation by his work in unearthing the Oklahoma "Gold Brick" land frauds.

Elliot leaves Seattle in the Queen City Thursday for the North, where he will make a thorough investigation of the whole situation with a view to clearing up the matter definitely. If his report is favorable to the claimants, the patents will be granted without further delay.

This was too good to keep. Holt pulled on his boots and went out to twit such of the enemy as he might meet. It chanced that the first of them was Selfridge, whom he had not seen since his arrival, though he knew the little man was in camp.

"How goes it, Holt? Fine and dandy, eh?" inquired Wally with the professional geniality he affected.

The old miner shook his head dolefully. "I done bust my laig, Mr. Selfish," he groaned. It was one of his pleasant ways to affect a difficulty of hearing and a dullness of understanding, so that he could legitimately call people by distorted versions of their names. "The old man don't amount to much nowadays. Onct a man or a horse gits stove up I don't reckon either one pans out much pay dust any more."

"Nothing to that, Gid. You're younger than you ever were, judging by your looks."

"Then my looks lie to beat hell, Mr. Selfish."

"My name is Selfridge," explained Wally, a trifle irritated.

Holt put a cupped hand to his ear anxiously. "Shellfish, did you say? Tha' 's right. How come I to forget? The old man's going pretty fast, Mr. Shellfish. No more memory than a jackrabbit. Say, Mr. Shellfish, what's the idee of all this here back-to-the-people movement, as the old sayin' is?"

"I don't know what you mean. And my name is Selfridge, I tell you," snapped the owner of that name.

" 'Course I ain't got no more sense than the law allows. I'm a buzzard haid, but me I kinder got to millin' it over and in respect to these here local improvements, as you might say, I'm doggoned if I *sabe* the whyfor." There was an imp of malicious deviltry in the black, beady eyes sparkling at Selfridge from between narrowed lids.

"Just some business changes we're making."

Holt showed his tobacco-stained teeth in a grin splenetic. "Oh. That's all. I didn't know but what you might be expecting a visitor."

Selfridge flashed a sharp sidelong glance at him. "What do you mean—a visitor?"

"I just got a notion mebbe you might be looking for one, Mr. Pelfrich. But I don't know sic' 'em. Like as not you ain't fixing up for this Gordon Elliot a-tall."

Wally had no come-back, unless it was one to retort in ironic admiration. "You're a wonder, Holt. Pity you don't start a detective bureau."

The old man went away cackling dryly.

If Selfridge had held any doubts before, he discarded them now. Holt would wreck the whole enterprise, were he given a chance. It would never do to let Elliot meet and talk with him. He knew too much, and he was eager to tell all he knew.

Macdonald's lieutenant got busy at once with plans to abduct Holt. That it was very much against the law did not disturb him much, so long as his chief stood back of him. The unsupported word of the old man would not stand in court, and if he became obstreperous they could always have him locked up as a lunatic. The very pose of the old miner—the make-believe pretension that he was half a fool—would lend itself to such a charge.

"We'll send the old man off on a prospecting trip with some of the boys," explained Selfridge to Howland. "That way we'll kill two birds. He's back on his assessment work. The time limit will be up before he returns and we'll start a contest for the claim."

Howland made no comment. He was an engineer and not a politician. In his position it was impossible for him not to know that a good deal about the legal status of the Macdonald claims was irregular. But he was a firm believer in a wide-open Alaska, in the use of the Territory by those who had settled it. The men back of the big Scotchman were going to spend millions in development work, in building railroads. It would help labor and business. The whole North would feel a healthful reaction from the Kamatlah activities. So, on the theory that the end sometimes justifies doubtful means, he shut his eyes to many acts that in his own private affairs he would not have countenanced.

"Better arrange it with Big Bill, then, but don't tell me anything about it. I don't want to know the details," he told Selfridge.

Big Bill Macy accepted the job with a grin. There was double pay in it both for him and the men he chose as his assistants. He had never liked old Holt anyhow. Besides, they were not going to do him any harm.

Holt was baking a batch of sour-dough bread that evening when there came a knock at the cabin door. At sight of Big Bill and his two companions the prospector closed the oven and straightened with alert suspicion. He was not on visiting terms with any of these men. Why had they come to see him? He asked point-blank the question in his mind.

"We're going prospecting up Wild-Goose Creek, and we want you to go along, Gid," explained Macy. "You're an old sour-dough miner, and we-all agree we'd like to have you throw-in with us. What say?"

The old miner's answer was direct but not flattering. "What do I want to go on a wild-goose mush with a bunch of bums for?" he shrilled.

Bill Macy scratched his hook nose and looked reproachfully at his host. At least Holt thought he was looking at him. One could not be sure, for Bill's eyes did not exactly track.

"That ain't no kind o' way to talk to a fellow

when he comes at you with a fair proposition, Gid."

"You tell Selfridge I ain't going to leave Kamatlah—not right now. I'm going to stay here on the job till that Land Office inspector comes—and then I'm going to have a nice, long, confidential chat with him. See?"

"What's the use of snapping at me like a turtle? Durden says Wild-Goose looks fine. There's gold up there—heaps of it."

"Let it stay there, then. I ain't going. That's flat." Holt turned to adjust the damper of his stove.

"Oh, I don't know. I wouldn't say that," drawled Bill insolently.

The man at the stove caught the change in tone and turned quickly. He was too late. Macy had thrown himself forward and the weight of his body flung Holt against the wall. Before the miner could recover, the other two men were upon him. They bore him to the floor and in spite of his struggles tied him hand and foot.

Big Bill rose and looked down derisively at his prisoner. "Better change your mind and go with us, Holt. We'll spend a quiet month up at the headquarters of Wild-Goose. Say you'll come along."

"You'll go to prison for this, Bill Macy."

"Guess again, Gid, and mebbe you'll get it right this time." Macy turned to his companions.

"George, you bring up the horses. Dud, see if that bread is cooked. Might as well take it along with us—save us from baking tomorrow."

"What are you going to do with me?" demanded Holt.

"I reckon you need a church to fall on you before you can take a hint. Didn't I mention Wild-Goose Creek three or four times?" jeered his captor.

"Every step you take will be one toward the penitentiary. Get that into your cocoanut," the old miner retorted sharply.

"Nothing to that idee, Gid."

"I'll scream when you take me out."

"Go to it. Then we'll gag you."

Holt made no further protest. He was furious, but at present quite helpless. However it went against the grain, he might as well give in until rebellion would do some good.

Ten minutes later the party was moving silently along the trail that led to the hills. The pack-horses went first, in charge of George Holway. The prisoner walked next, his hands tied behind him. Big Bill followed, and the man he had called Dud brought up the rear.

They wound up a rising valley, entering from it a cañon with precipitous walls that shut out the late sun. It was by this time past eleven o'clock and dusk was gathering closer. The winding trail ran parallel with the creek, sometimes through thickets of young fir and sometimes across boulder beds that made traveling difficult and slow. They went in single file, each of them with a swarm of mosquitoes about his head.

Macy had released the hands of his prisoner so that he might have a chance to fight the singing pests, but he kept a wary eye upon him and never let him move more than a few feet from him. The trail grew steeper as it neared the head of the canon till at last it climbed the left wall and emerged from the gulch to an uneven mesa.

The leader of the party looked at his watch. "Past midnight. We'll camp here, George, and see if we can't get rid of the 'skeeters."

They built smudge fires of green wood and on the lee side of these another one of dry sticks. Dud made coffee upon this and cooked bacon to eat with the fresh bread they had taken from the oven of Holt. While George chopped wood for the fires and boughs of small firs for bedding, Big Bill sat with a rifle across his knees just back of the prisoner.

"Gid's a shifty old cuss, and I ain't taking any chances," he explained aloud to Dud.

Holt was beginning to take the outrage philosophically. He sat close to a smudge and smoked his pipe.

"I wouldn't either if I were you. Sometime when you ain't watching, I'm liable to grab that gun and shoot a hole in the place where your brains would be if you had any," countered the old man.

He slept peacefully while they took turns watching him. Just now there would be no chance to escape, but in a few days they would become careless. The habit of feeling that they had him securely would grow upon them. Then, reasoned Holt, his opportunity would come. One of the guards would take a chance. Perhaps he might even fall asleep on duty. It was not reasonable to suppose that in the next week or two he would not catch them napping once for a short ten seconds.

There was, of course, just the possibility that they intended to murder him, but Holt could not associate Selfridge with anything so lawless. The man was too soft of fiber to carry through such a programme, and as yet there was need of nothing so drastic. No, this little kidnapping expedition would not run to murder. He would be set free in a few weeks, and if he told the true story of where he had been his foes would spread the report that he was insane in his hatred of Macdonald and imagined all sorts of persecutions.

They followed Wild-Goose Creek all next day, getting always closer to its headwaters near the divide. On the third day they crossed to the other side of the ridge and descended into a little mountain park. They were in a country where prospectors never came, one deserted even by trappers at this season of the year.

The country was so much a primeval wilderness that a big bull moose stalked almost upon their camp before discovering the presence of a strange biped. Big Bill snatched up a rifle and took a shot which sent the intruder scampering.

From somewhere in the distance came a faint sound.

"What was that?" asked George.

"Sounded like a shot. Mebbe it was an echo," returned Dud.

"Came too late for an echo," Big Bill said.

Again faintly from some far corner of the basin the sound drifted. It was like the pop of a scarcely heard firecracker.

The men looked at one another and at their prisoner. Their eyes consulted once more.

"Think we better break camp and drift?" asked Dud.

"No. We're in a little draw here—as good a hiding-place as we'd be likely to find. Drive the horses into the brush, George. We'll sit tight."

"Got the criminals guessing," Holt contributed maliciously. "You lads want to take the hide offen Macy if he lands you in the pen through that fool shot of his. Wonder if I hadn't better yell."

"I'll stop your clock right then if you do," threatened Big Bill with a scowl.

Dud had been busy stamping out the campfire

while Holway was driving the horses into the brush.

"Mebbe you had better get the camp things behind them big rocks," Macy conceded.

Even as he spoke there came the crack of a revolver almost at the entrance to the draw.

One of the men swore softly. The gimlet eyes of the old miner fastened on the spot where in another moment his hoped-for rescuers would appear.

A man staggered drunkenly into view. He reeled halfway across the mouth of the draw and stopped. His eyes, questing dully, fell upon the camp. He stared, as if doubtful whether they had played him false, then lurched toward the waiting group.

"Lost, and all in," Holway said in a whisper to Dud.

The other man nodded. Neither of them made a move toward the stranger, who stopped in front of their camp and looked with glazed eyes from one to another. His face was drawn and haggard and lined. Extreme exhaustion showed in every movement. He babbled incoherently.

"Seven—eighteen—ninety-nine. 'Atta-boy," he said thickly.

"Don't you see he's starving and out of his head?" snapped Holt brusquely. "Get him grub, *pronto*."

The old man rose and moved toward the

suffering man. "Come, pard. Tha' 's all right. Sit down right here and go to it, as the old sayin' is." He led the man to a place beside Big Bill and made him sit down. "Better light a fire, boys, and get some coffee on. Don't give him too much solid grub at first."

The famished man ate what was given him and clamored for more.

"Coming up soon, pardner," Holt told him soothingly. "Now tell us howcome you to get lost."

The man nodded gravely. "Hit that line low, Gord. Hit 'er low. Only three yards to gain."

"Plumb bughouse," commented Dud, chewing tobacco stolidly.

"Out of his head—that's all. He'll be right enough after he's fed up and had a good sleep. But right now he's sure some Exhibit A. Look at the bones sticking through his cheeks," Big Bill commented.

"Come, Old-Timer. Get down in your collar to it. Once more now. Don't lie down on the job. All together now." The stranger clucked to an imaginary horse and made a motion of lifting with his hands.

"Looks like his hawss bogged down in Fifty-Mile Swamp," suggested Holt.

"Looks like," agreed Dud.

The old miner said no more. But his eyes narrowed to shining slits. If this man had come through Fifty-Mile Swamp he must have started from the river. That probably meant that he had come from Kusiak. He was a young man, talking the jargon of a college football player. Without doubt he was, in the old phrasing of the North, a chechako. His clothing, though much soiled and torn, had been good. His voice held the inflections of the cultured world.

Gideon Holt's sly brain moved keenly to the possibility that he could put a name to this human derelict they had picked up. He began to see it as more than a possibility, as even a probability, at least as a fifty-fifty chance. A sardonic grin hovered about the corners of his grim mouth. It would be a strange freak of irony if Wally Selfridge, to prevent a meeting between him and the Government land agent, had sent him a hundred miles into the wilderness to save the life of Gordon Elliot and so had brought about the meeting that otherwise would never have taken place.

CHAPTER X
THE RAH-RAH BOY FUNCTIONS

Big Bill grumbled a good deal at the addition to the party. It would be decidedly awkward if this stranger should become rational and understand the status of the camp he had joined. The word of old Holt alone might be negligible, but supported by that of a disinterested party it would be a very different matter. Still, there was no help for it. They would have to take care of the man until he was able to travel. Perhaps he would go in with them as an additional guard. At the worst Big Bill could give him a letter to Selfridge explaining things and so pass the buck to that gentleman.

Gid Holt had, with the tacit consent of his guards, appointed himself as a sort of nurse to the stranger. He lit a smudge fire to the windward side of him, fed him small quantities of food at intervals, and arranged a sleeping-place for him with mosquito netting for protection.

Early in the evening the sick man fell into a sound sleep from which he did not awake until morning. George was away looking after the pack-horses, Dud was cooking breakfast, and Big Bill, his rifle close at hand, was chopping young firs fifty feet back of the camp. The cook also had a gun, loaded with buckshot, lying on a box beside him, so that they were taking no chances with their prisoner. He could not have covered twenty yards without being raked by a cross-fire.

The old miner turned from rearranging the boughs of green fir on the smudge to see that his patient was awake and his mind normal. The quiet, steady eyes resting upon him told that the delirium had passed.

"Pretty nearly all in, wasn't I?" the young man said.

The answer of Gid Holt was an odd one. "Yep. Seven—eleven—fifteen. Take 'er easy, old man," he said in his shrill, high voice as he moved toward the man in the blankets. Then, in a low tone, while he pretended to arrange the bedding over the stranger, he asked a quick question.

"Are you Elliot?"

"Yes."

"Don't tell them. Talk football lingo as if you was still out of your haid." Holt turned and called to Dud. "Says he wants some breakfast."

"On the way," the cook answered.

Holt seemed to be soothing the delirious man. What he really said was this. "Selfridge has arranged a plant for you at Kamatlah. The camp has been turned inside out to fool you. They've brought me here a prisoner so as to keep me from telling you the truth. Pst! Tune up now."

Big Bill had put down his axe and was

approaching. He was not exactly suspicious, but he did not believe in taking unnecessary chances.

"I tell you I'm out of training. Played the last game, haven't we? Come through with a square meal, you four-flusher," demanded Elliot in a querulous voice. He turned to Macy. "Look here, Cap. Haven't I played the game all fall? Don't I get what I want now we're through?"

The voice of the young man was excited. His eyes had lost their quiet steadiness and roved restlessly to and fro. If Big Bill had held any doubts one glance dissipated them.

"Sure you do. Hustle over and help Dud with the breakfast, Holt. I'll look out for our friend."

Elliot and Holt found no more chance to talk together that morning. Sometimes the young Government official lay staring straight in front of him. Sometimes he appeared to doze. Again he would talk in the disjointed way of one not clear in the head.

An opportunity came in the afternoon for a moment.

"Keep your eyes skinned for a chance to lay out the guard to-night and get his gun," Holt said quickly.

Gordon nodded. "I don't know that I've got to do everything just as you say," he complained aloud for the benefit of George, who was passing on his way to the place where the horses were hobbled.

"Now—now! There ain't nobody trying to boss you," Holt explained in a patient voice.

"They'd better not," snapped the invalid.

"Some scrapper—that kid," said the horse wrangler with a grin.

Macy took the first watch that night. He turned in at two after he had roused Dud to take his place. The cook had been on duty about an hour when Elliot kicked Holt, who was sleeping beside him, to make sure that he was ready. The old man answered the kick with another.

Presently Gordon got up, yawned, and strolled toward the edge of the camp.

"Don't go and get lost, young fellow," cautioned Dud.

Gordon, on his way back, passed behind the guard, who was sitting tailor fashion before a smudge with a muley shotgun across his knees.

"This ain't no country for chechakoes to be wandering around without a keeper," the cook continued. "Looks like your folks would have better sense than to let their rah-rah boy—"

He got no farther. Elliot dropped to one knee and his strong fingers closed on the gullet of the man so tightly that not even a groan could escape him. His feet thrashed to and fro as he struggled, but he could not shake off the grip that was strangling him. The old miner, waiting with every muscle ready and every nerve under tension, flung aside his blanket and hurled himself at the guard. It took him less time than it takes to tell to wrest the gun from the cook.

He got to his feet just as Big Bill, his eyes and brain still fogged with sleep, sat up and began to take notice of the disturbance.

"Don't move," warned Holt sharply. "Better throw your hands up. You reach for the stars, too, Holway. No monkey business, do you hear? I'd as lief blow a hole through you as not."

Big Bill turned bitterly upon Elliot. "So you were faking all the time, young fellow. We save your life and you round on us. You're a pretty slick proposition as a double-crosser."

"And that ain't all," chirped up Holt blithely. "Let me introduce our friend to you, Mr. Big Bill Macy. This is Gordon Elliot, the land agent appointed to look over the Kamatlah claims. Selfridge gave you lads this penitentiary job so as I wouldn't meet Elliot when he reached the camp. If he hadn't been so darned anxious about it, our young friend would have died here on the divide. But Mr. Selfridge kindly outfitted a party and sent us a hundred miles into the hills to rescue the perishing, as the old sayin' goes. Consequence is, Elliot and me meet up and have that nice confidential talk after all. The ways of Providence is strange, as you might say, Mr. Macy."

"Your trick," conceded Big Bill sullenly. "Now what are you going to do with us?"

117

"Not a thing—going to leave you right here to prospect Wild-Goose Creek, answered Holt blandly. "Durden says there's gold up here— heaps of it."

Bill Macy condemned Durden in language profane and energetic. He didn't stop at Durden. Holt came in for a share of it, also Elliot and Selfridge.

The old miner grinned at him. "You'll feel better now you've got that out of your system. But don't stop there if you'd like to say a few more well-chosen words. We got time a-plenty."

"Cut it out, Bill. That line o' talk don't buy you anything," said Holway curtly. "What's the use of beefing?"

"Now you're shouting, my friend," agreed old Gideon. "I guess, Elliot, you can loosen up on the chef's throat awhile. He's had persuading enough, don't you reckon? I'll sit here and sorter keep the boys company while you cut the pack-ropes and bring 'em here. But first I'd step in and unload all the hardware they're packing. If you don't one of them is likely to get anxious. I'd hate to see any of them commit suicide with none of their friends here to say, 'Don't he look natural?' "

Elliot brought back the pack-ropes and cut them into suitable lengths. Holt's monologue rambled on. He was garrulous and affable. Not for a long time had he enjoyed himself so much.

"Better begin with Chief Big Bill," he suggested. "No, I wouldn't make that move if I was you, Mr. Macy. This old gun is liable to go off accidental in your direction and she spatters like hell. That's the idee. Be reasonable. Not that I give a hoot, but a man hadn't ought to let his impulses run away with his judgment, as the old sayin' is."

Gordon tied the hands of Big Bill behind him, then roped his feet together, after which he did the same for Holway. The old miner superintended the job and was not satisfied till he had added a few extra knots on his own behalf.

"That'll hold them for awhile, I shouldn't wonder. Now if you'll just cover friend chef with this sawed-off gat, Elliot, I'll throw the diamond hitch over what supplies we'll need to get back to Kamatlah. I'll take one bronch and leave the other to the convicts," said Holt cheerfully.

"Forget that convict stuff," growled Macy. "With Macdonald back of us and the Guttenchilds back of him, you'll have a hectic time getting anything on us."

"That might be true if these folks were back of you. But are they? Course I ain't any Sherlock Holmes, but it don't look to me like they'd play any such fool system as this."

Big Bill opened his mouth to answer—and said nothing. He had caught a look flashed at him by Holway, a look that warned him he was talking too much.

After Holt had packed one of the animals he turned to Elliot.

"I reckon we're ready."

Under orders from Elliot, Dud fixed up the smudges and arranged the mosquito netting over the bound men so as to give them all the protection possible.

"We're going to take Dud with us for a part of the trip. We'll send him back to you later in the day. You'll have to fast till he gets back, but outside of that you'll do very well if you don't roll around trying to get loose. Do that, and you'll jar loose the mosquito netting. You know what that means," explained Gordon.

"It ain't likely any grizzlies will come pokin' their noses into camp. But you never can tell. Any last words you want sent to relatives?" asked Gideon Holt.

The last words they heard from Big Bill as they moved down the draw were sulphuric.

"Macy he ain't wearin' any W. J. Bryan smile this glad mo'nin'," mused old Holt aloud.

It was three o'clock in the morning by the watch when they started. About nine they threw off for breakfast. By this time they were just across the divide and were ready to take the down trail.

"I think we'll let Dud go now," Elliot told his partner in the adventure.

"Better hold him till afternoon. Then they can't possibly reach us till we get to Kamatlah."

"What does it matter if they do? We have both rifles and have left them only one revolver. Besides, I don't like to leave two bound men alone in so wild a district for any great time. No, we'll start Dud on the back trail. That grizzly you promised Big Bill might really turn up."

The two men struck the headwaters of Wild-Goose Creek about noon and followed the stream down. They traveled steadily without haste. So long as they kept a good lookout there was nothing to be feared from the men they had left behind. They had both a long start and the advantage of weapons.

If Elliot had advertised for a year he could not have found a man who knew more of Colby Macdonald's past than Gideon Holt. The old man had mushed on the trail with him in the Klondike days. He had worked a claim on Frenchman Creek with him and had by sharp practice—so at least he had come to believe—been lawed out of his rights by the shrewd Scotchman. For seventeen years he had nursed a grudge against Macdonald, and he was never tired of talking about him. He knew many doubtful things charged to the account of the big man as he had blazed a way to success over the failures of less fortunate people. One story in particular interested Gordon. It came out the second day, as they were getting down into the foothills.

"There was Farrell O'Neill. He was a good

fellow, Farrell was, but he had just one weakness. There was times when he liked the bottle too well. He'd let it alone for months and then just lap the stuff up. It was the time of the stampede to Bonanza Creek. Men are just like sheep. They wear wool on their backs like them and have their habits. You can start 'em any fool way for no cause a-tall. Don't you know it? Well, the news of the strike on Bonanza reached Dawson and we all burnt up the trail to get to the new ground first. O'Neill was one of the first. He got in about twenty below discovery, if I remember. Mac wasn't in Dawson, but he got there next mo'nin' and heard the news. He lit out for Bonanza *pronto*."

The old miner stopped, took a chew of tobacco, and looked down into the valley far below where Kamatlah could just be seen, a little huddle of huts.

"Well?" asked Elliot. It was occasionally necessary to prompt Holt when he paused for his dramatic effects. He would pretend to forget that he was telling a yarn which might interest his hearer.

"Mac draps in and joins O'Neill at night. They knew each other, y' understand, so o' course it was natural Mac would put up at his camp. O'Neill had a partner and they had located together. Fellow named Strong."

"Not Hanford Strong, a little, heavy-set man

somewhere around fifty?" Gordon asked quickly.

"You've tagged the right man. Know him?"

"I've met him."

"Well, I never heard anything against Han Strong. Anyway, he was off that night packing grub up while Farrell held down the claim. Mac had a jug of booze with him. He got Farrell tanked up. You know Mac—how he can put it across when he's a mind to. He's a forceful devil, and he can be a mighty likable one."

Elliot nodded understanding. "He's always the head of the table no matter where he sits. And there is something wonderfully attractive about him."

"Sure there is. But when he is friendliest you want to watch out he don't slip an upper cut at you that'll put you out of biz. He done that to Farrell—and done it a-plenty."

"How?"

"O'Neill got mellowed up till he thought Mac was his best friend. He was ready to eat out of his hand. So Mac works him up to sign a contract—before witnesses too; trust Mac for that—exchanging his half-interest in the claim for five hundred dollars in cash and Mac's no-'count lease on Frenchman Creek. Inside of a week Mac and Strong struck a big pay streak. They took over two hundred thousand from the spring clean-up."

"It was nothing better than robbery."

"Call it what you want to. Anyhow, it stuck. O'Neill kicked, and that's all the good it did him. He consulted lawyers at Dawson. Finally he got so discouraged that he plumb went to pieces—got on a long bat and stayed there till his money ran out. Then one bitter night he starts up to Bonanza to have it out with Mac. The mercury was so low it had run into the ground a foot. Farrell slept in a deserted cabin without a fire and not enough bedding. He caught pneumony. By the time he reached the claim he was a mighty sick man. Next week he died. That's all Mac done to O'Neill. Not a thing that wasn't legal either."

Gordon thought of Sheba O'Neill as she sat listening to the tales of Macdonald in Diane's parlor and his gorge rose at the man.

"But Mac had fell on his feet all right," continued Holt. "He got his start off that claim. Now he's a millionaire two or three times over, I reckon."

They reached the outskirts of Kamatlah about noon of the third day. Gordon left Holt at his cabin after they had eaten and went in alone to look the ground over. He met Selfridge at the post-office. That gentleman was effusive in his greeting.

"This *is* a pleasant surprise, Mr. Elliot. When did you get in? Had no idea you were coming or I'd have asked you for the pleasure of your

124

company. I'm down on business, of course. No need to tell you that—nobody would come to this hole for any other reason. Howland and his wife are the only possible people here. Hope you play bridge."

Elliot played it, but he did not say so. It was his business not to be drawn into entangling alliances.

"Of course you'll put up with me as my guest," Selfridge flowed on. "I've wanted to meet you again ever since we were on the Hannah together."

This was a little too cheeky. Gordon recalled with some amusement how this tubby little man and his friends had ignored the existence of Sheba O'Neill and himself for several days.

He answered genially. "Pleasant time we had on the river, didn't we? Thanks awfully for your invitation, but I've already made arrangements for putting up."

"Where? There's no decent place in camp except at Howland's. He keeps open house for our friends."

"I couldn't think of troubling him," countered Gordon.

"No trouble at all. We'll send for your things. Where are they?"

The land agent let him have it right between the eyes. "At Gideon Holt's. I'm staying with him on his claim."

Wally had struck a match to light a cigarette, but this simple statement petrified him. His jaw dropped and his eyes bulged. Not till the flame burned his fingers did he come to life.

"Did you say you were staying—with Gid Holt?" he floundered weakly.

Gordon noticed that his florid face had lost its color. The jaunty cock-sureness of the man had flickered out like the flame of the charred match.

"Yes. He offered to board me," answered the young man blandly.

"But—I didn't know he was here—seems to me I had heard—somewhere—that he was away."

"He was away. But he has come back." Gordon gave the information without even a flash of mirth in his steady eyes.

Selfridge could not quite let the subject alone. "Seems to me I heard he went prospecting."

"He did. Up Wild-Goose Creek, with Big Bill Macy and two other men. But I asked him to come back with me—and he did."

Feebly Wally groped for the clue without finding it. Had Big Bill sold him out? And how had Elliot got into touch with him?

"Just so, Mr. Elliot. But really, you know, Howland can make you a great deal more comfortable than Holt. His wife is a famous cook. I'll have a man go get your traps."

"It's very good of you, but I think I won't move."

"Oh, but you must. Holt's nutty—nobody at home, you know. Everybody knows that."

"Is he? The old man struck me as being remarkably clear-headed. By the way, I want to thank you for sending a relief party out to find me, Mr. Selfridge. Except for your help I would have died in the hills."

This was another facer for Wally. What the devil did the fellow mean? The deuce of it was that he knew all the facts and Wally did not. He talked as if he meant it, but behind those cool eyes there might lie either mockery or irony. One thing alone stood out to Selfridge like a sore thumb. His plans had come tumbling down like a house of cards. Either Big Bill had blundered amazingly, or he had played traitor. In either case Wally could guess pretty shrewdly whose hide Macdonald would tan for the failure. The chief wanted results. He did not ask of his subordinates how they got them. And this was the second time in succession that Selfridge had come to grief.

CHAPTER XI
GORDON INVITES HIMSELF TO DINNER—AND DOES NOT ENJOY IT

Big Bill and his companions reached Kamatlah early next day. They reported at once to Selfridge. It had been the intention of Wally to vent upon them the bad temper that had been gathering ever since his talk with Elliot. But his first sarcastic question drew such a snarl of anger that he reconsidered. The men were both sullen and furious. They let him know roundly that if Holt made them any trouble through the courts, they would tell all they knew.

The little man became alarmed. Instead of reproaches he gave them soft words and promises. The company would see them through. It would protect them against criminal procedure. But above all they must stand pat in denial. A conviction would be impossible even if the State's attorney filed an indictment against them. Meanwhile they would remain on the company payroll.

Gordon Elliot was a trained investigator. Even without Holt at his side he would probably have unearthed the truth about the Kamatlah situation. But with the little miner by his side to tell him the facts, he found his task an easy one.

Selfridge followed orders and let him talk with the men freely. All of them had been drilled till they knew their story like parrots. They were suspicious of the approaches of Elliot, but they had been warned that they must appear to talk candidly. The result was that some talked too much and some not enough. They contradicted themselves and one another. They let slip admissions under skillful examination that could be explained on no other basis than that of company ownership.

Both Selfridge and Howland outdid themselves in efforts to establish close social relations. But Gordon was careful to put himself under no obligations. He called on the Howlands, but he laughingly explained why he could not accept the invitations of Mrs. Howland to dinner.

"I have to tell things here as I see them, and may not have your point of view. How can I accept your hospitality and then report that I think your husband ought to be sent up for life?"

She was a good, motherly woman and she laughed with him. But she did wish this pleasant young fellow could be made to take the proper view of things.

Within two weeks Elliot had finished his work at Kamatlah.

"Off for Kusiak to-morrow," he told Holt that night.

The old miner went with him as a guide to the big bend. Gordon had no desire to attempt again Fifty-Mile Swamp without the help of some one who knew every foot of the trail. Holt had taken the trip a dozen times. With him to show the way the swamp became merely a hard, grueling mush through boggy lowlands.

Weary with the trail, they reached the river at the end of a long day. An Indian village lay sprawled along the bank, and through this the two men tramped to the roadhouse where they were to put up for the night.

Holt called to the younger man, who was at the time in the lead.

"Wait a minute, Elliot."

Gordon turned. The old Alaskan was offering a quarter to a little half-naked Indian boy. Shyly the four-year-old came forward, a step at a time, his finger in his mouth. He held out a brown hand for the coin.

"What's your name, kid?" Holt flashed a look at Elliot that warned him to pay attention.

"Colmac," the boy answered bashfully.

His fist closed on the quarter, he turned, and like a startled caribou he fled to a comely young Indian woman standing near the trail.

With gleaming eyes Holt turned to Elliot. "Take a good look at the squaw," he said in a low voice.

Elliot glanced at the woman behind whose

skirts the youngster was hiding. He smiled and nodded pleasantly to her.

"She's not bad looking if that's what you mean," he said after they had taken up the trail again.

"You ain't the only white man that has thought that," retorted the old miner significantly.

"No?" Gordon had learned to let Holt tell things at his leisure. It usually took less time than to try to hurry him.

"Name of the kid mean anything to you?"

"Can't say it did."

"Hm! Named for his dad. First syllable of each of his names."

The land inspector stopped in his stride and wheeled upon Holt. His eyes asked eagerly a question. "You don't mean Colby Macdonald?"

"Why don't I?"

"But—Good Lord, he isn't a squawman, is he?"

"Not in the usual meaning of the word. She never cooked and kept house for him. Just the same, little Colmac is his kid. Couldn't you see it sticking out all over him? He's the spit'n' image of his dad."

"I see it now you've pointed it out. I was trying to think who he reminded me of. Of course it was Macdonald."

"Mac met up with Meteetse when he first scouted this country for coal five years ago. So far's I know he was square enough with the girl.

132

She never claimed he made any promises or anything like that. He sends a check down once a quarter to the trader here for her and the kid."

But young Elliot was not thinking about Meteetse. His mind's eye saw another picture—the girl at Kusiak, listening spellbound to the tales of a man whose actions translated romance into life for her, a girl swept from the quiet backwaters of an Irish village to this land of the midnight sun with its amazing contrasts.

And all the way up on the boat she continued to fill his mind. The slowness of the steamer fretted him. He paced up and down the deck for hours at a time worried and anxious. Sometimes the jealousy in his heart flamed up like a prairie fire when it comes to a brush heap. The outrage of it set him blazing with indignation. Diane ought to be whipped, he told himself, for her part in the deception. It was no less than a conspiracy. What could an innocent young girl like Sheba know of such a man as Colby Macdonald? Her imagination conceived, no doubt, an idealized vision of him. But the real man was clear outside her ken.

Gordon set his jaw grimly. He would have it out with Diane. He would let her see she was not going to have it all her own way. By God, he would put a spoke in her wheel.

Sometimes, when the cool, evening breezes blew on his bare, fevered head, he laughed at himself for an idiot. How did he know that Macdonald wanted Sheba O'Neill. All the evidence he had was that he had once seen the man watch her while she sang a sentimental song. Whereas it was common talk that he would probably marry Mrs. Mallory, that for months he had been her almost daily companion. If the older woman had lost the sweet, supple slimness of her first youth, she had won in exchange a sophisticated grace, a seductive allure that made her the envy of all the women with whom she associated. She held at command a warm, languorous charm which had stirred banked fires in the hearts of many men. Why should not Macdonald woo her? Gordon himself admitted her attractiveness.

And why should he take it for granted that Sheba was ready to drop into the arms of the big Alaskan whenever he said the word? At the least he was twenty years older than she. Surely she might admire him without falling in love with the man. Was there not something almost insulting in the supposition that Macdonald had only to speak to her in order to win?

But in spite of reason he was on fire to come to his journey's end. No sooner had he reached his hotel than he called up Mrs. Paget. Quite clearly she understood that he wanted an invitation to dinner. Yet she hesitated.

"My 'phone can't be working well," Gordon told her gayly. "You must have asked me to

134

dinner, but I didn't just hear it. Never mind. I'll be there. Seven o'clock, did you say?"

Diane laughed. "You're just as much a boy as you were ten years ago, Gord. All right. Come along. But you're to leave at ten. Do you understand?"

"No, I can't hear that. My 'phone has gone bad again. And if I had heard, I shouldn't think of doing anything so ridiculous as leaving at that hour. It would be an insult to your hospitality. I know when I'm well off."

"Then I'll have to withdraw my invitation. Perhaps some other day—"

"I'll leave at ten," promised Elliot meekly.

He could almost hear the smile in her voice as she answered. "Very well. Seven sharp. I'll explain about the curfew limit sometime."

Macdonald was with Miss O'Neill in the living-room when Gordon arrived at the Paget home.

Sheba came forward to greet the new guest. The welcome in her eyes was very genuine.

"You and Mr. Macdonald know each other, of course," she said after her handshake.

The Scotchman nodded his lean, grizzled head, looking straight into the eyes of the field agent. There was always a certain deliberation about his manner, but it was the slowness of strength and not of weakness.

"Yes, I know Mr. Elliot—now. I'm not so sure that he knows me—yet."

135

"I'm beginning to know you rather well, Mr. Macdonald," answered Gordon quietly, but with a very steady look.

If the Alaskan wanted to declare war he was ready for it. The field agent knew that Selfridge had sent reports detailing what had happened at Kamatlah. Up to date Macdonald had offered him the velvet glove. He wondered if the time had come when the fist of steel was to be doubled.

Paget was frankly pleased to see Gordon again. He was a simple, honest man who moved always in a straight line. He had liked Elliot as a boy and he still liked him. So did Diane, for that matter, but she was a little on her guard against him. She had certain plans under way that she intended to put through. She was not going to let even Gordon Elliot frustrate them.

"Did you have a successful trip, Mr. Elliot?" asked Sheba innocently.

Paget grinned behind his hand. The girl's question was like a match to powder, and every one in the room knew it but she. The engineer's interests and his convictions were on the side of Macdonald, but he recognized that Elliot had been sent in to gather facts for the Government and not to give advice to it. If he played fair, he could only tell the truth as he saw it.

The eyes of Diane held a spark of hostility as she leaned forward. The word had already been passed among the faithful that this young man was not taking the right point of view.

"Did you, Gordon?" echoed his hostess.

"I think so," he answered quietly.

"I hear you put up with old Gideon Holt. Is he as cracked as he used to be?" asked Macdonald.

"Was he cracked when you used to know him on Frenchman Creek?" countered the young man.

Macdonald shot a quick, slant look at him. The old man had been talking, had he?

"He was cracked and broke too," laughed the mine-owner hardily. "Cracked when he came, broke when he left."

"Yes, that was one of the stories he told me." Gordon turned to Sheba. "You should meet the old man, Miss O'Neill. He knew your father at Dawson and on Bonanza."

The girl was all eagerness. "I'd like to. Does he ever come to Kusiak?"

"Nonsense!" cut in Diane sharply. She flashed at Gordon a look of annoyance. "He's nothing but a daft old idiot, my dear."

The dinner had started wrong, and though Paget steered the conversation to safer ground, it did not go very well. At least three of those present were a little on edge. Even Sheba, who had missed entirely the point of the veiled thrusts, knew that Elliot was not in harmony with either Diane or Macdonald.

Gordon was ashamed of himself. He could not

137

quite have told what were the impulses that had moved him to carry the war into the camp of the enemy. Perhaps, more than anything else, it had been a certain look of quiet assurance in the eyes of his rival when he looked at Sheba.

He rose promptly at ten.

"Must you go so soon?" Diane asked. She was smiling at him with bland mockery.

"I really must," answered Elliot.

His hostess followed him into the hall. She watched him get into his coat before saying what was on her mind.

"What did you mean by telling Sheba that old Holt knew her father? What is he to tell her if they meet—that her father died of pneumonia brought on by drink? Is that what you want?"

Gordon was honestly contrite. "I didn't think of that."

"No, you were too busy thinking of something mean to say to Mr. Macdonald."

He agreed, yet could not forbear one dig more. "I suppose I wanted Holt to tell her that Macdonald robbed her father and indirectly was the cause of his death."

"Absurd!" exploded Diane. "You're so simple that you accept as true the gossip of every crack-brained idiot—when it suits your purpose."

He smiled, boyishly, engagingly, as he held out his hand. "Don't let's quarrel, Di. I admit I forgot myself."

"All right. We won't. But don't believe all the catty talk you hear, Gordon."

"I'll try to believe only the truth." He smiled, a little ruefully. "And it isn't necessary for you to explain why the curfew law applies to me and not to Macdonald."

She was on her dignity at once. "You're quite right. It isn't necessary. But I'm going to tell you anyhow. Mr. Macdonald is going away tomorrow for two or three days and he has some business he wants to talk over with Sheba. He had made an appointment with her, and I didn't think it fair to let your coming interfere with it."

Gordon took this facer with his smile still working.

"I've got a little business I want to talk over with *you*, Di."

She had always been a young woman of rather a hard finish. Now she met him fairly, eye to eye. "Any time you like, Gordon."

Elliot carried away with him one very definite impression. Diane intended Sheba to marry Macdonald if she could bring it about. She had as good as served notice on him that the girl was spoken for.

The young man set his square jaw. Diane was used to having her own way. So was Macdonald. Well, the Elliots had a will of their own too.

CHAPTER XII
SHEBA SAYS "PERHAPS"

Obeying the orders of the general in command, Peter took himself to his den with the excuse that he had blue-prints to work over. Presently Diane said she thought she heard one of the children crying and left to investigate.

The Scotchman strode to the fireplace and stood looking down into the glowing coals. He seemed in no hurry to break the silence and Sheba glanced at his strong, brooding face a little apprehensively. Her excitement showed in the color that was beating into her cheeks. She knew of only one subject that would call for so formal a private talk between her and Macdonald, and any discussion of this she would very much have liked to postpone.

He turned from the fire to Sheba. It was characteristic of him that he plunged straight at what he wanted to say.

"I've asked to see you alone, Miss O'Neill, because I want to make a confession and restitution—to begin with," he told her abruptly.

She had a sense of suddenly stilled pulses. "That sounds very serious." The young woman smiled faintly.

His face of chiseled granite masked all emotion. It kept under lock and key the insurgent impulses that moved him when he looked into the sloe eyes charged with reserve. Back of them, he felt, was the mystery of purity, of maidenhood. He longed to know her better, to find out and to appropriate for himself the woman that lay behind the fine veil of flesh. She seemed to him delicate as a flame and as vivid. There would come a day when her innocent, passional nature would respond to the love of a man as a waiting harp does to skillful fingers.

"My story goes away back to the Klondike days. I told you that I knew your father on Frenchman Creek, but I didn't say much about knowing him on Bonanza."

"Mr. Strong has told me something about the days on Bonanza, and I knew you would tell me more some day—when you wanted to speak about it." She was seated in a low chair and the white throat lifted toward him was round as that of a bird.

"Your father was among the first of those who stampeded to Bonanza. He and Strong took up a claim together. I bought out the interest of your father."

"You told me that."

His masterful eyes fastened to hers. "I didn't tell you that I took advantage of him. He was—not well. I used that against him in the bargaining.

He wanted ready money, and I tempted him."

"Do you mean that you—wronged him?"

"Yes. I cheated him." He was resolved to gloss over nothing, to offer no excuses. "I didn't know there was gold on his claim, but I had what we call a hunch. I took his claim without giving value received."

It was her turn now to look into the fire and think. From the letters of her father, from talks with old-timers she knew how in the stampedes every man's hand had been for himself, how keen-edged had been the passion for gold, a veritable lust that corroded the souls of men.

"But—I don't understand." Her brave, steady eyes looked directly into those of Macdonald. "If he felt you had—done him a wrong—why did he come to you when he was ill?"

"He was coming to demand justice of me. On the way he suffered exposure and caught pneumonia. The word reached us, and Strong and I brought him to our cabin."

"You faced a blizzard to bring him in. Mr. Strong told me how you risked your life by carrying him through the storm—how you wouldn't give up and leave him, though you were weak and staggering yourself. He says it was a miracle you ever got through."

The big mine-owner brushed this aside as of no importance. "We don't leave sick men to die in a blizzard up North. But that's not the point."

"I think it has a bearing on the matter—that you saved him from the blizzard—and took him in—and nursed him like a brother till he died."

"I'm not heartless," said Macdonald impatiently. "Of course I did that. I had to do it. I couldn't do less."

"Or more," she suggested. "You may have made a hard bargain with him, but you wiped that out later."

"That's just what I didn't do. Don't think my conscience is troubling me. I'm not such a mushbrained fool. If it had not been for you I would never have thought of it again. But you are his daughter. What I cheated him out of belongs to you—and you are my friend."

"Don't use that word about what you did, please. He wasn't a child. If you got the best of him in a bargain, I don't think father would think of it that way."

The difficulty was that he could not tell her the truth about her father's weakness for drink and how he had played upon it. He bridged all explanations and passed to the thing he meant to do in reparation.

"The money I cleaned up from that claim belongs to you, Miss O'Neill. You will oblige me by taking it."

From his pocket he took a folded paper and handed it to her. Sheba opened it doubtfully. The paper contained a typewritten statement and to it was attached a check by means of a clip. The check was made out to her and signed by Colby Macdonald. The amount it called for was one hundred and eighty-three thousand four hundred and thirty-one dollars.

"Oh, I couldn't take this, Mr. Macdonald—I couldn't. It doesn't belong to me," she cried.

"It belongs to you—and you're going to take it."

"I wouldn't know what to do with so much."

"The bank will take care of it for you until you decide. So that's settled." He passed definitely from the subject. "There's something else I want to say to you, Miss O'Neill."

Some change in his voice warned her. The girl slanted a quick, shy glance at him.

"I want to know if you'll marry me, Miss O'Neill," he shot at her abruptly. Then, without giving her time to answer, he pushed on: "I'm older than you—by twenty-five years. Always I've lived on the frontiers. I've had to take the world by the throat and shake from it what I wanted. So I've grown hard and willful. All the sweet, fine things of life I've missed. But with you beside me I'm not too old to find them yet— if you'll show me the way, Sheba."

A wave of color swept into her face, but her eyes never faltered from his. "I'm not quite sure," she said in a low voice.

"You mean—whether you love me?"

She nodded. "I—admire you more than any man I ever met. You are a great man, strong and powerful,—and I am so insignificant beside you. I—am drawn to you—so much. But—I am not sure."

Afterward, when she thought of it, Sheba wondered at the direct ease of his proposal. In the romances she had read, men were shy and embarrassed and fearful of the issue. But Colby Macdonald had known what he wanted to say and had said it as coolly and as readily as if it had been a business detail. She was the one that had blushed and stammered and found a difficulty in expressing herself.

"I'm going away for two days. Perhaps when I come back you will know, Sheba. Take your time. Marriage is serious business. I want you to remember that my life has been very different from yours. You'll hear all sorts of things about me. Some of them are true. There is this difference between a man and a good woman. He fights and falls and fights again and wins. But a good woman is finer. She has never known the failure that drags one through slime and mud. Her goodness is born in her; she doesn't have to fight for it."

The girl smiled a little tremulously. "Doesn't she? We're not all angel, you know."

"I hope you're not. There will need to be a lot of the human in you to make allowances for

Colby Macdonald," he replied with an answering smile.

When he said good-bye it was with a warm, strong handshake.

"I'll be back in two days. Perhaps you'll have good news for me then," he suggested.

The dark, silken lashes of her eyes lifted shyly to meet his.

"Perhaps," she said.

CHAPTER XIII
DIANE AND GORDON DIFFER

During the absence of Macdonald the field agent saw less of Sheba than he had expected, and when he did see her she had an abstracted manner he did not quite understand. She kept to her own room a good deal, except when she took long walks into the hills back of the town. Diane had a shrewd idea that the Alaskan had put his fortune to the test, and she not only let her cousin alone herself, but fended Gordon from her adroitly.

The third day after the dinner Elliot dropped around to the Pagets with intent to get Sheba into a set of tennis. Diane sat on the porch darning socks.

"Sheba is out walking with Mr. Macdonald," she explained in answer to a question as to the whereabouts of her guest.

"Oh, he's back, is he?" remarked Gordon moodily.

Mrs. Paget was quite cheerful on that subject. "He came back this morning. Sheba has gone up with him to see the Lucky Strike."

"You're going to marry her to that man if you can, aren't you?" he charged.

"If I can, Gordon." She slipped a darning-ball

into one of little Peter's stockings and placidly trimmed the edges of the hole.

"It's what I call a conspiracy."

"Is it?" Diane smiled.

Gordon understood her smile to mean that he was jealous.

"Maybe I am. That's not the point," he answered, just as if she had made her accusation in words.

"Suppose you tell me what the point is," she suggested, both amused and annoyed.

"He isn't good enough for her. You know that perfectly well."

"Good enough!" She shrugged her shoulders. "What man *is* good enough for a nice girl if you come to that? There are other things beside sugary goodness. Any man who is strong can make himself good enough for the woman he loves."

"Generally speaking, yes. But Colby Macdonald is different."

"Thank Heaven he is," she retorted impatiently. Then added after a moment: "He isn't a Sunday-School superintendent if that's what you mean."

"That isn't what I mean at all. But there's such a thing as a difference between right and wrong, isn't there?"

"Oh, yes. For instance, Mr. Macdonald is right about the need of developing Alaska and the way to do it, and you are wrong."

He could not help smiling a little at the adroit way she tried to sidetrack him, even though he was angry at her. But he had no intention of letting her go without freeing his mind.

"I'm talking about essential right and wrong. Miss O'Neill is idealizing Macdonald. I don't suppose you've told her, for instance, that he made his first money in the North running a dance hall."

"No, I haven't told her any such thing, because it isn't true," she replied scornfully. "He owned an opera house and brought in a company of players. I dare say they danced. That's very different, as you'd know if you didn't have astigmatism of the mind."

"Not the way the story was told me. But let that pass. Does she know that Macdonald beat her father out of one of the best claims on Bonanza and was indirectly responsible for his death?"

"What's the use of talking nonsense, Gordon. You know you can't prove that," his friend told him sharply.

"I think I can—if it is necessary."

Diane looked across at him with an impudent little tilt of the chin. "I don't think I like you as well as I used to."

"Sorry, because I'd like you just as well, Diane, if you would stop trying to manage your cousin into a marriage that will spoil her life," he answered gravely.

151

"How dare you say that! How dare you, Gordon Elliot!" she flung back, furious at him. "I won't have you here talking that way to me. It's an insult."

The fearless, level eyes of her friend looked straight at her. "I say it because the happiness of Miss O'Neill is of very great importance to me."

"Do you mean—?" Wide-eyed, she looked her question straight at him.

"That's just what I mean, Diane."

She darned for a minute in silence. It had occurred to Diane before that perhaps Gordon might be in love with Sheba, but she had put the thought from her because she did not want to believe it.

"That's different, Gordon. It explains—and in a way excuses—your coming here and trying to bully me." She stopped her work to flash a question at him. "Don't you think that maybe it's only a fancy of yours? I remember you used—"

He shook his head. "No chance, Diane. I'm hard hit. She's the only girl I ever met that suited me. Everything she does is right. Every move she makes is wonderful."

The eyes with which she looked at him were softer, as those of women are wont to be for the true romance.

"You poor boy," she murmured, and let her hand for a moment rest on his.

"Meaning that I lose?" he asked quickly.

"I think you do. I'm not sure."

Elliot leaned forward impulsively. "Be a good sport, Diane. Let me have my chance too. Why do you make it easy for Macdonald and hard for me? Isn't it because the glamour of his millions blinds you?"

"He's a big, splendid man, but I don't like him any the less because he has the power to make life easy and comfortable for Sheba," she defended sturdily.

"Yet you turned down Arthur West, the best catch in your set, to marry Peter, who was the worst," he reminded her. "Have you ever been sorry for it?"

"That's different. Peter and I fit. It was one case out of a million." She gave him her old, friendly smile. "But I don't want to be hard on you, Gord. I'll be neutral. Come and see Sheba as often as she'll let you."

Gordon beamed as he shook hands with her, "That sounds like the Di Paget I used to know."

She recurred to the previous question. "Sheba knows more about Mr. Macdonald than you think. And about how he got her father's claim, for instance,—she has heard all that."

"You told her?"

"No. Colby Macdonald told her. He said he practically robbed her father, and he gave her a check for nearly two hundred thousand to cover the clean-up from the claim and interest."

"Bully for him." On the heel of this he flung a question at her. "Did Macdonald ask her to marry him the night of the dinner?"

A flash of whimsical amusement lit her dainty face. "You'd better ask him that. Here he comes now."

They were coming down the walk together, Macdonald and Sheba. The young woman was absorbed in his talk, and she did not know that her cousin and Elliot were on the porch until she was close upon them. But at sight of the young man her eyes became warm and kind.

"I'm sorry I was out yesterday when you called," she told him.

"And you were out again to-day. My luck isn't very good, is it?"

He laughed pleasantly, but his heart was bitter. He believed Macdonald had won. Some hint of proprietorship in his manner, together with her slight confusion when she saw them on the porch, had weighted his heart with lead.

"We've had such a good walk." Sheba went on quickly. "I wish you could have heard Mr. Macdonald telling me how he once had a chance to save a small Esquimaux tribe during a hard winter. He carried food five hundred miles to them. It was a thrilling experience."

"Mr. Macdonald has had a lot of very inter-esting experiences. You must get him to tell you about all of them," answered Gordon quietly.

The eyes of the two men met. The steel-gray ones of the older man answered the challenge of his rival with a long, steady look. There was in it something of triumph, something of scornful insolence. If this young fellow wanted war, he did not need to wait long for it.

"Time enough for that, man. Miss O'Neill and I have the whole Arctic winter before us for stories."

The muscles in the lean jaws of Gordon Elliot stood out like steel ropes. He turned to Sheba. "Am I to congratulate Mr. Macdonald?"

The color in her cheeks grew warmer, but her shy glance met his fairly. "I think it is I that am to be congratulated, Mr. Elliot."

Diane took her cousin in her arms. "My dear, I wish you all the happiness in the world," she said softly.

The Irish girl fled into the house as soon as she could, but not before making an announcement.

"We're to be married soon, very quietly. If you are still at Kusiak we want you to be one of the few friends present, Mr. Elliot."

Macdonald backed her invitation with a cool, cynical smile. "Miss O'Neill speaks for us both, of course, Elliot."

The defeated man bowed. "Thanks very much. The chances are that I'll be through my business here before then."

As soon as his fiancée had gone into the

house, the Scotchman left. Gordon sat down in a porch chair and stared straight in front of him. The suddenness of the news had brought his world tumbling about his ears. He felt that such a marriage would be an outrage against Sheba's innocence. But he was not yet far enough away from the blow to ask himself how much the personal hurt influenced his opinion.

Though she was sorry for him, Diane did not think it best to say so yet.

Presently he spoke thickly. "I suppose you have heard that he was a squawman."

His friend joined battle promptly with him. "That's ridiculous. Don't be absurd, Gordon."

"It's the truth. I've seen the woman. She was pointed out to me."

"By old Gideon Holt, likely," she flashed.

"One could get evidence and show it to Miss O'Neill," he said aloud, to himself rather than to her.

Diane put her point of view before him with heated candor. "*You* couldn't. Nobody but a cad would rake up old scandals about the man who has beaten him fairly for a woman's love."

"You beg the question. *Has* he won fairly?"

"Of course he has. Be a good sport, Gordon. Don't kick on the umpire's decision. Play the game."

"That's all very well. But what about her? Am I to sit quiet while she is sacrificed to a code of honor that seems to me rooted in dishonor?"

"She is not being sacrificed. I'm her cousin. I'm very fond of her. And I'd trust her with Colby Macdonald."

"Play fair, Diane. Tell her the truth about this Indian woman and let your cousin decide for herself. You can't do less, can you?"

Mrs. Paget was distinctly annoyed. "You ought to be ashamed of yourself, Gordon Elliot. You take all the gossip of a crack-brained old idiot for gospel truth just because you want to believe the worst about Mr. Macdonald. Don't you know that people will say anything about a man who succeeds? Colby Macdonald is too big and too aggressive not to have made hundreds of enemies. His life has been threatened dozens of times. But he pays no attention to it—goes right on building-up this country. Yet you'd think he had a cloven hoof to hear some people talk. I've no patience with them."

"The woman's name is Meteetse," Gordon said in an even voice, just as if he were answering a question. "She is young and good-looking for an Indian. Her boy is four or five years old. Colmac, they call him, and he looks just like Macdonald."

"People are always tracing resemblances. There's nothing to that. But suppose his life *was* irregular—years ago. This isn't Boston. It used to be the fringe of civilization. Men did as they pleased in the early days. We don't ask a man up here what he has been, but what he is. You ought to know that by this time."

"This wasn't in the early days. It was five years ago, when Macdonald was examining the Kamatlah coal-field. I'm told he sends a check down the river once a month for the woman."

"All the more credit to him if he does." Diane rose and looked stormily down at her friend. "You're about as broad as a clam, Gordon. Can't you see that even if it's true, all that is done with? It is a part of his past—and it's finished—trodden under foot. It hasn't a thing to do with Sheba."

"I don't agree with you. A man can't cut loose entirely from his past. It is a part of him—and Macdonald's past isn't good enough for Sheba O'Neill."

Diane tapped her little foot impatiently on the floor. "Do you know many men whose pasts are good enough for their wives? Are you a plaster-cast saint yourself? You know perfectly well that men trample down their pasts and begin again when they are married. Colby Macdonald is good enough for any woman alive if he loves her enough."

"You don't know him."

"I know him far better than you do. He is the biggest man I know, and now that he is in love with a good woman he'll rise to his chance."

"She ought to be told the truth about Meteetse and her boy," he insisted doggedly.

"I'm not going to disturb her with a lot of old maids' gossip. That's flat."

"But if I prove to you that it isn't gossip."

Mrs. Paget lost her temper completely. "Does the Government pay you to mind other people's business, Gordon?" she snapped.

"I wouldn't be working for the Government then, but for Sheba O'Neill."

"And for Gordon Elliot. You'd be doing underhand work for him too. Don't forget that. You can't do it. You're not that kind of a man. It isn't in you to go muckraking in the past of the man Sheba is going to marry."

Elliot rose and looked across at the blue-ribbed mountains. His square jaw was set when he turned it back toward Diane.

"She isn't going to marry him if I can help it," he said quietly.

He walked out of the gate and down the walk toward his hotel.

A message was waiting for him there from his chief in Seattle. It called him down the river on business.

CHAPTER XIV
GENEVIEVE MALLORY
TAKES A HAND

Inside of an hour the news of the engagement of Macdonald was all over Kusiak. It was through a telephone receiver that the gossip was buzzed to Mrs. Mallory by a friend who owed her a little stab. The voice of Genevieve Mallory registered faint amusement, but as soon as she had hung up, her face fell into haggard lines. She had staked a year of her waning youth on winning the big mining man of Kusiak, together with all the money that she had been able to scrape up for a campaign outfit. Moreover, she liked him.

It was not in the picture that she should fall desperately in love with any man. A woman of the world, she was sheathed in the plate armor of selfishness. But she was as near to loving Macdonald as was possible for her. She had a great deal of admiration for his iron strength, for the grit of the man. No woman could twist him around her finger, yet it was possible to lead him a long way in the direction one wanted.

Mrs. Mallory sat down in the hall beside the telephone, her fingers laced about one crossed knee. She knew that if Sheba O'Neill had not come on the scene, Macdonald would have asked her to marry him. He had been moving slowly toward her for months. They understood each other and were at ease together. Between them was a strong physical affinity. Both were good-tempered and were wise enough to expect human imperfection.

Then Diane Paget had brought in this slim, young cousin of hers and Colby Macdonald had been fascinated by the mystery of her innocent youth. Mrs. Mallory was like steel beneath the soft and indolent surface. Swiftly she mapped her plan of attack. The Alaskan could not be moved, but it might be possible to startle the girl into breaking the engagement. Genevieve Mallory would have used the weapon at hand without scruple in any case, but she justified herself on the ground that such a marriage could result only in unhappiness.

But before she made any move Mrs. Mallory intended to be sure of her facts. It was like her to go to headquarters for information. She got Macdonald on the wire.

"I've just heard something nice about you. Do tell me it's true," she said, her voice warm with sympathy.

Macdonald laughed with an almost boyish embarrassment. "It's true, I reckon."

"I'm so glad. She's a lovely girl. The sweetest thing that ever lived. I'm sure you'll be happy.

I always did think you would make a perfect husband. Of course, I'm simply green with envy of her."

Her little ripple of laughter was gay and carefree. The man at the other end of the line never had liked her better. Since he was not a fool he had guessed pretty closely how things stood with her. She was a game little sport, he told himself approvingly. It appealed to him immensely that she could take such a facer and come up smiling.

There were no signs of worry wrinkles on her face when the maid admitted a caller half an hour later. Oliver Dustin was the name on the card. He was a remittance man, a tame little parlor pet whose vocation was to fetch and carry for pretty women, and by some odd trick of fate he had been sifted into the Northland. Mrs. Mallory had tolerated him rather scornfully, but today she smiled upon him.

Propped up by pillows, she reclined luxuriously on a lounge. A thin spiral of smoke rose like incense to the ceiling from her lips. The slow, regular rise and fall of her breathing beneath the filmy lace of her gown accented the perfect fullness of bust and throat.

Dustin helped himself to a cigarette and made himself comfortable.

She set herself to win him. He was immensely flattered at her awakened interest. When she called him by his first name, he wagged all over like a pleased puppy.

It came to him after a time that she was considering him for a confidential mission. He assured her eagerly that there was no trouble too great for him to take if he could be of any service to her. She hesitated and doubted and at last as a special favor to him accepted his offer. Their heads were close in whispered talk for a few minutes, at the end of which Dustin left the room with his chin in the air. He was a knight errant in the employ of the most attractive woman north of fifty-three.

When Elliot took the down-river boat he found Oliver Dustin was a fellow passenger. The little man smoked an occasional cigar with the land agent and aired his views on politics and affairs social. He left the boat at the big bend. Without giving him much of his thought Gordon was a little surprised that the voluble remittance man had not told him where he was going.

Not till a week later did Elliot return up the river. He was asleep at the time the Sarah passed the big bend, but next morning he discovered that Selfridge and Dustin had come aboard during the night. In the afternoon he came upon a real surprise when he found Meteetse and her little boy Colmac seated upon a box on the lower deck where freight for local points was stored.

His guess was that they were local passengers, but wharf after wharf slipped behind them and the two still remained on board. They appeared to know nobody else on the Sarah, though once Gordon met Dustin just as he was hurrying away from the Indian woman. The little remittance man took the pains to explain to Elliot later that he was trying to find out whether the Indians knew any English.

Meteetse transferred with the other Kusiak passengers at the river junction. The field agent was not the only one on board who wondered where she was going. Selfridge was consumed with curiosity, and when she and the boy got off at Kusiak, he could restrain himself no longer. Gordon saw Wally talking with her. Meteetse showed him an envelope which evidently had an address written upon it, for the little man pointed out to her the direction in which she must go.

Since leaving Kusiak nearly two weeks before, no word had reached Gordon of Sheba. As soon as he had finished dinner at the hotel, he walked out to the Paget house and sent in his card.

Sheba came into the hall to meet him from the living-room where she had been sitting with the man she expected to marry next week. She gave a little murmur of pleasure at sight of him and held out both hands.

"I was afraid you weren't going to get back in time. I'm so glad," she told him warmly.

He managed to achieve a smile. "When is the great day?"

"Next Thursday. Of course, we're as busy as can be, but Diane says—"

A ring at the door interrupted her. Sheba stepped forward and let in an Indian woman with a little boy clinging to her hand.

"You Miss O'Neill?" she asked.

"Yes."

From the folds of her shawl she drew a letter. The girl glanced at the address, then opened and read what was written. She looked up, puzzled, first at the comely, flat-footed Indian woman and afterward at the handsome little brown-faced papoose. She turned to Gordon.

"This letter says I am to ask this woman who is the father of her boy. What does it mean?"

Gordon knew instantly what it meant, though he could not guess who had dealt the blow. He hesitated for an answer, and in his embarrassment she felt that which began to ring a bell of warning in her heart.

The impulse to spare her pain was stronger in him than the desire that she should know the truth.

"Send her away," he urged. "Don't ask any questions. She has been sent to hurt you."

A fawnlike fear flashed into the startled eyes. "To hurt me?"

"I am afraid so."

"But—why? I have done nobody any harm." She seemed to hold even her breathing in suspense. Only a pulse beat wildly in her white throat like the heart of an imprisoned thrush.

"Perhaps some of Macdonald's enemies," he suggested.

And at that there came a star-flash into the soft eyes and a lifted tilt to the chin cut fine as a cameo. She turned proudly to the Indian woman.

"What is it that you have to tell me about this boy's father?"

Meteetse began to speak. At the first mention of Macdonald's name Sheba's eyes dilated. Her smile, her sweet, glad pleasure at Gordon's arrival, were already gone like the flame of a blown candle. Clearly her heart was a-flutter, in fear of she knew not what. When the Indian woman told how she had first crossed the path of Macdonald, the color flamed into the cheeks of the Irish girl, but as the story progressed, the blood ebbed even from her lips.

With a swift movement of her fingers she flashed on the hall light. Her gaze searched the brown, shiny face of the little chap. She read there an affidavit of the truth of his mother's tale. The boy had his father's trick of squinting a slant look at anything he found interesting. It was impossible to see him and not recognize Colby Macdonald reincarnated.

"What is your name?" asked Sheba suddenly.

The youngster hung back shyly among the

folds of the Indian woman's skirt. "Colmac," he said at last softly.

"Come!" Sheba flung open the door of the living-room and ushered them in.

Macdonald, pacing restlessly up and down the room during her absence, pulled up in his stride. He stood frowning at the native woman, then his eyes passed to Elliot and fastened upon him. The face of the Scotchman might have been chipped from granite. It was grim as that of a hanging judge.

Gordon started to explain, then stopped with a shrug. What was the use? The man would never believe him in the world.

"I'll remember this," the Alaskan promised his rival. There was a cold glitter in his eyes, a sudden flare of the devil that was blood-chilling.

"It's true, then," broke in Sheba. "You're a—a squawman. You belong to this woman."

"Nothing of the kind," he cried roughly. "That's been ended for years."

"Ended?" Sheba drew Colmac forward by the wrist. "Do you deny that this is your boy?"

The big Alaskan brushed this aside as of no moment. "I dare say he is. Anyhow I'm paying for his keep. What of it? That's all finished and done with."

"How can it be done with when—when she's the mother of your child, your wife before God?"

The live eyes attacked him from the dusk that framed the oval of her pale face. Standing there straight as an aspen, the beautiful bosom rising and falling quickly while the storm waves beat through her blood, Sheba O'Neill had never made more appeal to the strong, lawless man who desired her for his wife.

"You don't understand." Macdonald's big fists were clenched so savagely that the knuckles stood out white from the brown tan of the flesh. "This is a man's country. It's new—close to nature. What he wants he takes—if he's strong enough. I'm elemental. I—"

"You wanted her—and you took her. Now you want me—and I suppose you'll take me too." Her scornful words had the sting of a whiplash.

"I've lived as all men live who have red blood in them. This woman is an incident. I've been aboveboard. She can't say I ever promised more than I've given. I've kept her and the boy. It's been no secret. If you had asked, I would have told you the whole story."

"Does that excuse you?"

"I don't need any excuse. I'm a man. That's excuse enough. You've been brought up among a lot of conventions and social lies. The one big fact you want to set your teeth into now is that I love you, that there isn't another woman on God's earth for me, and that there never will be again."

Her eyes flashed battle. "The one big fact I'm facing is that you have insulted me—that you insult me again when you mention love with that woman and boy in the room. You belong to them—go to them—and leave me alone." She had been fighting for self-control, to curb her growing resentment, but now it flamed passionately into words. "I hate the sight of you. Why don't you go—all of you—and leave me in peace?"

It was a cry of bruised pride and wounded love. Elliot touched the Indian woman on the shoulder. Meteetse turned stolidly and walked out of the room, still leading Colmac by the hand. The young man followed.

Macdonald closed the door behind them, then strode frowning up and down the room. The fear was growing on him that for all his great driving power he could not shake this slim girl from the view to which she clung. If the situation had not been so serious, it would have struck him as ridiculous. His relation with Meteetse had been natural enough. He believed that he had acted very honorably to her. Many a man would have left her in the lurch to take care of the youngster by herself. But he had acknowledged his obligation. He was paying his debt scrupulously, and because of it the story had risen to confront him. He felt that it was an unjust blow of fate. Punishment was falling upon him, not for what he had done, but because he had scorned to make a secret of it.

He knew that he must justify himself before Sheba or lose her. As she stood in the dusk so tall and rigid, he knew her heart was steel to him. Her finely chiseled face had the look of race. Never had the spell of her been more upon him. He crushed back a keen-edged desire to take her supple young body into his arms and kiss her till the scarlet ran into her cheeks like splashes of wine.

"You haven't the proper slant on this, Sheba. Alaska is the last frontier. It's the dropping-off place. You're north of fifty-three."

"Am I north of the Ten Commandments?" she demanded with the inexorable judgment of youth. "Did you leave the moral code at home when you came in over the ice?"

He smiled a little. "Morality is the average conduct of the average man at a given time and place. It is based on custom and expediency. The rules made for Drogheda won't fit Dawson or Nome. The laws made to protect young women in Ireland would be absurd if applied to half-breed squaws in Alaska. Meteetse does not hold herself disgraced but honored. She counts her boy far superior to the other youngsters of the village, and he is so considered by the tribe. I am told she lords it over her sisters."

A faint flush of anger had crept into her cheeks.

"Your view of morality puts us on a level with the animals. I will not discuss the subject, if you please."

"We must discuss it. I must get you to see that Meteetse and what she stood for in my life have nothing to do with us. They belong to my past. She doesn't exist for either of us—isn't in any way a part of my present or future."

"She exists for me," answered Sheba listlessly. She felt suddenly old and weary. "But I can't talk about it. Please go. I want to be alone."

Again Macdonald paced restlessly down the room and back. He moved with a long, easy, tireless stride. The man was one among ten thousand, dominant, virile, every ounce of him strong as tested steel. But he felt as if all his energy were caged.

"Why don't you go?" the girl pleaded. "It's no use to stay."

He stopped in front of her. "I'm going to marry you, Sheba. Don't think I'll let that meddler interfere with our happiness. You're mine."

"No. Never!" she cried. "I'll take the boat and go home first."

"You've promised to marry me. You're going to keep your word and be glad of it all your life."

She shook her head. "No."

"Yes." Macdonald had always shown remarkable restraint with her. He had kissed her seldom, and always with a kind of awe at her young purity. Now he caught her by the shoulders. His eyes, deep in their sockets, mirrored the passionate desire of his heart.

The color flamed into her face. She looked hot to the touch, an active volcano ready to erupt. There was an odd feeling in her mind that this big man was a stranger to her.

"Take your hands from me," she ordered.

"Do you think I'm going to give you up now— now, after I've won you—because of a damfool scruple in your pretty head? You don't know me. It's too late. I love you—and I'm going to protect both of us from your prudishness."

His arms closed on her and he crushed her to him, looking down hungrily into the dark, little face.

"Let me go," she cried fiercely, struggling to free herself.

For answer he kissed the red lips, the flaming cheeks, the angry eyes. Then, coming to his senses, he pushed her from him, turned, and strode heavily from the room.

CHAPTER XV
GORDON BUYS A REVOLVER

Selfridge was not eager to meet his chief, but he knew he must report at once. He stopped at his house only long enough to get into fresh clothes and from there walked down to the office. Over the Paget telephone he had got into touch with Macdonald who told him to wait at headquarters until he came.

It had been the intention of Macdonald to go direct from Sheba to his office, but the explosion brought about by Meteetse had sent him out into the hills for a long tramp. He was in a stress of furious emotion, and until he had worked off the edge of it by hard mushing, the cramped civilization of the town stifled him.

Hours later he strode into the office of the company. He was dust-stained and splashed with mud. Fifteen miles of stiff heel-and-toe walking had been flung behind him.

Wally lay asleep in a swivel chair, his fat body sagging and his head fallen sideways in such a way as to emphasize the plump folds of his double chin. His eyes opened. They took in his chief slowly. Then, in a small panic, he jumped to his feet.

175

"Must 'a' been taking thirty winks," he explained. "Been up nights a good deal."

"What doing?" demanded the Scotchman harshly.

In a hurried attempt to divert the anger of Macdonald, his assistant made a mistake. "Say, Mac! Who do you think came up on the boat with me? I wondered if you knew. Meteetse and her kid—"

He stopped. The big man was glaring savagely at him. But Macdonald said nothing. He waited, and under the compulsion of his forceful silence Wally stumbled on helplessly.

"—They got off here. 'Course I didn't know whether you'd sent for her or not, so I stopped and kinder gave her the glad hand just to size things up."

"Yes."

"She had the address of Miss O'Neill, that Irish girl staying at the Pagets, the one that came in—"

"Go on," snapped his chief.

"So I directed her how she could get there and—"

Wally found himself lifted from the chair and hammered down into it again. His soft flesh quaked like a jelly. As he stared pop-eyed at the furious face above him, the fat chin of the little man drooped.

"My God, Mac, don't do that!" he whined.

Macdonald wheeled abruptly away, crossed the room in long strides, and came back. He had a grip on himself again.

"What's the use?" he said aloud. "You're nothing but a spineless putterer. Haven't you enough sense even to give me a chance to decide for myself? Why didn't you keep the woman with you till you could send for me, you daft donkey?"

"I swear I never thought of that."

"What have you got up there in your head instead of brains? I send you outside to look after things and you fall down on the job. I give you plain instructions what to do at Kamatlah and you let Elliot make a monkey of you. You see him on the boat with a woman coming to make trouble for me, and the best you can do is to help her on the way. Man, man, use your gumption."

"If I had known—"

"D'ye think you've got sense enough to take a plain, straight message as far as the hotel? Because if you have, I've got one to send."

Wally caressed tenderly his bruised flesh. He had a childlike desire to weep, but he was afraid Macdonald would kick him out of the office.

"'Course I'll do whatever you say, Mac," he answered humbly.

The Scotch-Canadian brushed the swivel chair and its occupant to one side, drew up another chair in front of the desk, and faced Selfridge squarely. The eyes that blazed at the little man were the grimmest he had ever looked into.

"Go to the hotel and see this man Elliot alone. Tell him he's gone too far—butted into my affairs once too often. There's not a man alive I'd stand it from. My orders are for him to get out on the next boat. If he's here after that, I'll kill him on sight."

The color ebbed out of the florid face of Wally. He moistened his lips to speak. "Good God, Mac, you can't do that. He'll go out and report—"

"To hell with his report. Let him say what he likes. Put this to him straight: that he and I can't stay in this town—*and both of us live.*"

Wally had lapped up too many highballs in the past ten years to relish this kind of a mission. He had depressed his nerves with overmuch tobacco and spurred them with liquors, had dissipated his force in many small riotings. His nerve was gone. He had not the punch any more. Yet Mac was always expecting him to help out with his rough stuff, he reflected fretfully. This was the third time in a month that he had been flung headlong into trouble. Take this message now. There was no sense in it. Selfridge plucked up his courage to say so.

"That won't buy us anything but trouble, Mac. In the old days you could put over—"

The little man never guessed how close he came to being flung through the transom over the door, but his instinct warned him to stop. His objection died away in a mumble.

"O' course I'll do whatever you say," he added a second time.

"See you do," advised his chief, an ugly look in his eyes. "Tell him he gets till the next boat. If he's here after that, he'd better go heeled, for I'll shoot on sight wherever we meet."

Selfridge went on his errand with lagging feet. On the way he stopped at the Pay-Streak Saloon to fortify himself with a cocktail. He found Elliot sitting moodily alone on the porch of the hotel.

In Gordon's pocket there was a note to Macdonald explaining that he had nothing to do with the coming of Meteetse. He had expected to send it by the hotel porter that evening, but the curt order to leave town filled him with a chill anger. The dictator of affairs at Kusiak might think what he pleased for all the explanation he would get from him. As for taking the next boat, Elliot did not even give that consideration.

"Tell your master I don't take orders from him," he told Wally quietly. "I'll stay till my work here is done."

They had moved a few yards down the street. Now Gordon turned, lean-loined and active, and trod with crisp, confident step back to the hotel. He had said all that was necessary to say.

Two men standing on the porch nodded a good-

179

evening to him. Gordon, about to pass, glanced at them again. They were Northrup and Trelawney, two of the miners who had had trouble with Macdonald on the boat.

On impulse he stopped. "Found work yet?" he asked.

"Found a job and lost it again," Northrup answered sullenly.

"Too bad."

"Macdonald passed the word along that we weren't to get work. So our boss fired us. The whole district is closed to us. We been black-listed," explained Trelawney.

"And we're busted," added his mate.

Elliot was always free-handed. Perhaps he felt just now unusually sympathetic towards these victims of the high-handed methods of Macdonald. From his pocket he took a small leather purse and gave a piece of gold to each of them.

"Just as a loan to carry you for a couple of days till you get something to do," he suggested.

Northrup demurred, but after a little pressure accepted the accommodation.

"I pay you soon back," he promised.

Trelawney laughed recklessly. He had been drinking.

"You bet. Me too."

His companion flashed a look of warning at him and explained that they were going down the river to look for work outside of the district.

Suddenly Trelawney broke loose and began to curse Macdonald with a bitterness that surprised the Government agent. What struck him most, though, was the obvious anxiety of Northrup to quiet his partner and to gloss over what he had said. Thinking of it later, Gordon wondered why the Dane, who had as much cause to hate Macdonald as the other, should be at such pains to smooth down the man and explain away his threats.

Elliot bought an automatic revolver next morning and a box of cartridges. He was not looking for trouble, but he intended to be prepared for it when trouble came looking for him. With a rifle he was a fair shot, but he lacked experience with the revolver. In the afternoon he walked out of town and practiced shooting at tin cans for a half an hour. On his way back he met Peter Paget.

The engineer came straight to the subject in his mind.

"Selfridge came to see me last night. He told me about the trouble between you and Macdonald, Gordon. You must leave town till he cools down. Macdonald is a bad man with a gat."

"Is he?"

"You can drop down the river on business for a few weeks. After a while—"

His friend looked at him coolly. "I can, but I'm

not going to. Where do you get this stuff about me being a quitter, Pete?"

Peter laid a hand on his shoulder. "Now, look here, Gordon. Don't be a kid and foolhardy. Duck. I'm your friend—"

"You're his, too, aren't you?"

"Yes, of course, but—"

"All right. Tell him to duck. There'll be no trouble of my making. But if he starts any I'll be there. Macdonald doesn't own the earth, you know. I've been sent up here by Uncle Sam on business, and you can bet your last dollar I'll stay on the job till I'm through."

"Of course you've got to finish your job. But it doesn't all have to be done right here. Just for a week or two—"

"Tell your friend something else while you're on the subject. If I drop him, I go scot free because he is interfering with me in my duty. I'll put Selfridge on the stand to prove it. But if he should kill me, his last chance for getting the Macdonald claims patented would be gone. The public would raise such a howl that the Administration would have to throw your friend and the Guttenchilds overboard to save itself. I know that—and Macdonald knows it. So he stands to lose either way."

Paget knew this was true. He knew, too, there was no use in arguing with this young athlete. That close-gripped jaw and salient chin did not belong to a slacker. Gordon would stick and see the thing out. But Peter could not drop the subject without one more appeal.

"He's not sore at you about the claims. You know that. It's because you brought the squaw up the river to see Sheba."

"I didn't bring her—hadn't a thing to do with that. I don't know who brought her, though I could give a good guess."

A gleam of hope showed in the eye of the engineer. "You didn't bring her? Diane said you threatened—"

"Maybe I did say I would. Anyhow, I thought better of it. But I'm glad some one had the sense to tell Miss O'Neill the truth."

"Who do you think brought her?"

"I'm not thinking on that subject out loud."

"But if we could show Mac—"

"That's up to you. I'll not lift a finger. Your king of Kusiak has to learn some time that everybody isn't going to sidestep him and pussyfoot when he's around. I didn't start this war and I'm not making any peace overtures."

"You're as obstinate as the devil," smiled Peter, but in his heart he admired the dourness of his friend.

The engineer went to Macdonald and gave a deleted version of his talk with Elliot. The Scotchman listened, a bitter, incredulous smile on his face.

"Says he didn't bring her, does he? Tell him from me that he lies. Your wife let out to me by accident that he threatened to bring her. Meteetse and he came up on the boat together. He was with her at your house when she told her story. He's trying to save his hide. No chance."

"Elliot isn't a liar. When he says he didn't bring the woman, that satisfies me. I know he didn't do it," insisted Paget stiffly.

"Different here. Who else had any interest in bringing her except him? Nobody. Use your brains, Peter. He takes the first boat down the river. He comes back on the next one. She comes back, too. They couldn't figure I'd be at your house when they showed up there to tell the story. That's where Mr. Elliot slipped up"

Peter was of different stuff from Selfridge. He had something to say. So he said it.

"Times have changed, Mac. You can't shoot down this young fellow without making all kinds of trouble. First thing we'd lose the claims. The Administration would drop you like a hot potato if you did a thing like that. Sheba would never speak to you again. Your friends would know in their hearts it was murder. You can't do it."

Macdonald's jaw clamped. "Then let him get out. That's my last word to him."

CHAPTER XVI
AMBUSHED

Colby Macdonald, in miner's boots and corduroy working suit, stood beside his horse with one arm thrown carelessly across its rump. He was about to start for Seven-Mile Creek Camp with twenty-seven hundred dollars in the saddlebags to pay the men there.

Diane was talking with him. "She's young and fine and spirited. Of course it was a great shock to her. She had been idealizing you. But I think she is beginning to understand things better. At any rate, she does not hate you any more. Give the girl time."

"You think she will—be reasonable?"

Mrs. Paget finished the pattern she was punching in the soft ground beside the board walk with the ferrule of her umbrella. Her eyes met his frankly.

"I don't know. But I'm sure of one thing. She'll not be reasonable, as you call it, unless you are reasonable."

"You mean—Elliot?"

"Yes. She likes him very much. Do you know that when the Indian woman came he urged Sheba not to listen to her story?"

"Sounds likely—after he had spent his good money bringing her here," sneered the mine-owner.

"He didn't. Gordon is a splendid fellow. He wouldn't lie," answered Diane hotly. "And one thing is sure—if you lay a finger on him for this, it will be fatal with Sheba. She will be through with you."

Macdonald had thought of this before. It had been coming to him from several different angles that he could not afford to gratify his desire to wipe this meddlesome young official from his path. He made a slow, sulky promise.

"All right. I'll let him alone. Peter can tell him."

Swinging to the saddle, he spurred his horse and cantered away. With a little smile Diane watched his flat, muscular back and the arrogant set of his strong shoulders. There was not his match in the territory, she thought, but sometimes a clever woman could manage him.

His mind was full of the problem that had come into his life. He rode abstractedly, so that he was at the lower ford of the creek almost before he knew it. A bilberry thicket straggled down to the opposite bank of the stream on both sides of the road.

The horse splashed through the ford and took the little rise beyond with a rush. Just before reaching the brow of the hill, the animal stumbled and fell. As its rider went headlong, he caught a glimpse of a cord drawn taut across the path.

Macdonald, shaken by the fall, began slowly to rise. From the shadows of the bilberry bushes two stooping figures rushed at him. He threw up an arm to ward off the club aimed at his head, but succeeded only in breaking the force of the blow. As he staggered back, stunned, a bullet glanced along his forehead and ridged a furrow through the thick hair. A second stroke of the club jarred him to the heels.

Though his mind was not clear, his body answered automatically the instinct that told him to close with his assailants. He lurched forward and gripped one, wrestling with him for the revolver. Vaguely he knew by the sharp, jagged shoots of pain that the second man was beating his head with a club. The warm blood dripped through his hair and blinded his eyes. Dazed and shaken, he yet managed to get the revolver from the man who had it. But it was his last effort. He was too far gone to use it. A blow on the forehead brought him unconscious to the ground bleeding from a dozen wounds.

On his way back from Seven-Mile Creek Camp Gordon Elliot rode down to the ford. In the dusk he was almost upon them before the robbers heard him. For a moment the two men stood gazing at him and he at the tragedy before him. One of the men moved toward his horse.

"Stop there!" ordered Gordon sharply, and he reached for his revolver.

The man—it was the miner Northrup—jumped for Elliot and the field agent fired. Another moment, and he was being dragged from the saddle. What happened next was never clear to him. He knew that both of the bandits closed in on him and that he was fighting desperately against odds. The revolver had been knocked from his hand and he fought with bare fists just as they did. Twice he emptied his lungs in a cry for help.

They quartered over the ground, for Gordon would not let either of them get behind him. They were larger than he, heavy, muscle-bound giants of great strength, but he was far more active on his feet. He jabbed and sidestepped and retreated. More than once their heavy blows crashed home on his face. His eyes dared not wander from them for an instant, but he was working toward a definite plan. As he moved, his feet were searching for the automatic he had dropped.

One of his feet, dragging over the ground came into contact with the steel. With a swift side kick Gordon flung the weapon a dozen feet to the left. Presently, watching his chance, he made a dive for it.

Trelawney, followed by Northrup, turned and ran. One of them caught Macdonald's horse by the bridle. He swung to the saddle and the other man clambered on behind. There was a clatter of hoofs and they were gone.

Elliot stooped over the battered body that lay huddled at the edge of the water. The man was either dead or unconscious, he was not sure which. So badly had the face been beaten and hammered that it was not until he had washed the blood from the wounds that Gordon recognized Macdonald.

Opening the coat of the insensible man, Gordon put his hand against the heart. He could not be sure whether he felt it beating or whether the throbbing came from the pulses in his fingertips. As well as he could he bound up the wounds with handkerchiefs and stanched the bleeding. With ice-cold water from the stream he drenched the bruised face. A faint sigh quivered through the slack, inert body.

Gordon hoisted Macdonald across the saddle and led the horse through the ford. He walked beside the animal to town, and never had two miles seemed to him so far. With one hand he steadied the helpless body that lay like a sack of flour balanced in the trough of the saddle.

Kusiak at last lay below him, and when he descended the hill to the suburbs almost the first house was the one where the Pagets lived.

Elliot threw the body across his shoulder and walked up the walk to the porch. He kicked upon the door with his foot. Sheba answered the knock, and at sight of what he carried the color faded from her face.

"Macdonald has been hurt—badly," he explained quickly.

"This way," the girl cried, and led him to her own room, hurrying in advance to throw back the bedclothes.

"Get Diane—and a doctor," ordered Gordon after he had laid the unconscious man on the white sheet.

While he and Diane undressed the mine-owner Sheba got a doctor on the telephone. The wounded man opened his eyes after a long time, but there was in them the glaze of delirium. He recognized none of them. He did not know that he was in the house of Peter Paget, that Diane and Sheba and his rival were fighting with the help of the doctor to push back the death that was crowding close upon him. All night he raved, and his delirious talk went back to the wild scenes of his earlier life. Sometimes he swore savagely; again he made quiet deadly threats; but always his talk was crisp and clean and vigorous. Nothing foul or slimy came to the surface in those hours of unconscious babbling.

The doctor had shaken his head when he first saw the wounds. He would make no promises.

"He's a mighty sick man. The cuts are deep, and the hammering must have jarred his brain terribly. If it was anybody but Macdonald, I

190

wouldn't give him a chance," he told Diane when he left in the morning to get breakfast. "But Macdonald has tremendous vitality. Of course if he lives it will be because Mr. Elliot brought him in so soon."

Gordon walked with the doctor as far as the hotel. A brown, thin, leathery man undraped himself from a chair in the lobby when Elliot opened the door. He was officially known as the chief of police of Kusiak. Incidentally he constituted the whole police force. Generally he was referred to as Gopher Jones on account of his habit of spasmodic prospecting.

"I got to put you under arrest, Mr. Elliot," he explained.

The loafers in the hotel drew closer.

"What for?" demanded Gordon, surprised.

"Doc thinks it will run to murder, I reckon."

The field agent was startled. "You mean—Macdonald?"

The brown man chewed his quid steadily. "You done guessed it."

"That's absurd, you know. What evidence have you got?"

"First off, you'd had trouble with him. It was common talk that when you and Mac met, guns were going to pop. You bought an automatic revolver at the Seattle & Kusiak Emporium two days ago. You was seen practicing with it."

"He had threatened me."

191

"You want to be careful what you say, Mr. Elliot. It will be used against you." Gopher shot a squirt of tobacco unerringly at the open door of the stove. "You was seen talking with Trelawney and Northrup. Money passed from you to them."

"I gave them a loan of ten dollars each because they were broke. Is that criminal?" demanded Gordon angrily.

"That's your story. You'll git a chance to tell it to the jury, I shouldn't wonder. Mebbe they'll believe it. You never can tell."

"Believe it! Why, you muttonhead, I found him where he was bleeding to death and brought him in."

"That's what I heard say. Kinder queer, ain't it, you happened to be the man that found him?"

"Nothing queer about it. I was riding in from Seven-Mile Creek Camp." Gordon was exasperated, but not at all alarmed.

"So you was. While you was out at the camp, you asked one of the boys how big the payroll would be."

"Does that prove I was planning a hold-up? Isn't that the last thing I would have asked if I had intended robbery?"

"Don't ask me. I ain't no psychologist. All I know is you took an interest in the bank-roll on the way."

"I'm here for the Government investigating

Macdonald. I was getting information—earning my pay. Can you understand that?"

Gopher chewed his cud impassively. "Sure I can, and I been earning mine. By the way, howcome you to be beat up so bad, Mr. Elliot?"

"I had a fight with the robbers."

"Sure it wasn't with the robbed. That split lip of yours looks to me plumb like Mac's John Hancock."

Elliot flushed angrily. "Of course if you intend to believe me guilty—"

"Now, there ain't no manner o' use in gettin' het up, young fellow. Mebbe you did it; mebbe you didn't. Anyhow, you'll gimme that gat you been toting these last few days."

Gordon's hand moved toward his hip. Then he remembered.

"I haven't it. I left it—"

"You left it at the ford—with one shell empty. That's where you left it," interrupted the officer.

"Yes. I fired at Northrup as he rushed me."

"Um-hu," assented Jones, impudent unbelief in his eye. "At Northrup or at Macdonald."

"What do you think I did with the money, then? Did I eat it?"

"Not so you could notice it. Since you put it to me flat-foot, you gave it to your pardners. You didn't want it. They did. They have got the horse too—and they're hitting the high spots to make their get-away."

193

Elliot was locked up in the flimsy jail without breakfast. He was furious, but as he paced up and down the narrow beat beside the bed his anger gave way to anxiety. Surely the Pagets could not believe he had done such a thing. And Sheba—would she accept as true this weight of circumstantial evidence that was piling up against him?

It could all be explained so easily. And yet—the facts fitted like links of a chain to condemn him. He went over them one by one. The babbling tongue of Selfridge that had made common gossip of the impending tragedy in which he and Macdonald were the principals—his purchase of the automatic—his public meeting with two known enemies of the Scotchman, during which he had been seen to give them money—his target practice with the new revolver—the unhappy chance that had taken him out to Seven-Mile Creek Camp the very day of the robbery—his casual questions of the miners—even the finding of the body by him. All of these dovetailed with the hypothesis that his partners in crime were to escape and bear the blame, while he was to bring the body back to town and assume inno-cence.

Paget was admitted to his cell later in the morning by Gopher Jones. He shook hands with the prisoner. Jones retired.

"Tough luck, Gordon," the engineer said.

"What does Sheba think?" asked the young man quickly.

"We haven't told her you have been arrested. I heard it only a little while ago."

"And Diane?"

"Yes, she knows."

"Well?" demanded Gordon brusquely.

Peter looked at him in questioning surprise. "Well, what?" He caught the meaning of his friend. "Try not to be an ass, Gordon. Of course she knows the charge is ridiculous."

The chip dropped from the young man's shoulder. "Good old Diane. I might have known," he said with a new cheerfulness.

"I think you might have," agreed Peter dryly. "By the way, have you had any breakfast?"

"No. I'm hungry, come to think of it."

"I'll have something sent in from the hotel."

"How's Macdonald?"

"He's alive—and while there's life there is hope."

"Any news of the murderers?" asked Gordon.

"Posses are combing the hills for them. They stole a packhorse from a truck gardener up the valley. It seems they bought an outfit for a month yesterday—said they were going prospecting."

They talked for a few minutes longer, mainly on the question of a lawyer and the chances of getting out on bond. Peter left the prisoner in very much better spirits than he had found him.

CHAPTER XVII
"GOD SAVE YOU KINDLY"

A nurse from the hospital had relieved Diane and
Sheba at daybreak. They slept until the middle of
the afternoon, then under orders from the doctor
walked out to take the air. They were to divide
the night watch between them and he said that
he wanted them fit for service. The fever of the
patient was subsiding. He slept a good deal, and
in the intervals between had been once or twice
quite rational.

The thoughts of the cousins drew their steps
toward the jail. Sheba looked at Diane.

"Will they let us see him, do you think?"

"Perhaps. We can try."

Gopher Jones was not proof against the brisk
confidence with which Mrs. Paget demanded
admittance. He stroked his unshaven chin while
he chewed his quid, then reluctantly got his
keys.

The prisoner was sitting on the bed. His heart
jumped with gladness when he looked up.

Diane shook hands cheerfully. "How is the
criminal?"

"Better for hearing your kind voice," he
answered.

197

His eyes strayed to the ebon-haired girl in the background. They met a troubled smile, grave and sweet.

"Awfully good of you to come to see me," he told Sheba gratefully. "How is Macdonald?"

"Better, we hope. He knew Diane this afternoon."

Mrs. Paget did most of the talking, but Gordon contributed his share. Sheba did not say much, but it seemed to the young man that there was a new tenderness in her manner, the expression of a gentle kindness that went out to him because he needed it. The walk had whipped the color into her cheeks and she bloomed in that squalid cell like a desert rose. There was in the fluent grace of the slender, young body a naive, virginal sweetness that took him by the throat. He knew that she believed in him and the trouble rolled from his heart like a cold, heavy wave.

"We haven't talked to Mr. Macdonald yet about the attack on him," Diane explained. "But he must have recognized the men. There are many footprints at the ford, showing how they moved over the ground as they fought. So he could not have been unconscious from the first blow."

"Unless they were masked he must have known them. It was light enough," agreed Elliot.

"Peter is still trying to get the officers to accept bail, but I don't think he will succeed. There is a good deal of feeling in town against you."

"Because I am supposed to be an enemy to an open Alaska, I judge."

"Mainly that. Wally Selfridge has been talking a good deal. He takes it for granted that you are guilty. We'll have to wait in patience till Mr. Macdonald speaks and clears you. The doctor won't let us mention the subject to him until he comes to it of his own free will."

Gopher stuck his head in at the door. "You'll have to go, ladies. Time's up."

When Sheba bade the prisoner good-bye it was with a phrase of the old Irish vernacular. "God save you kindly."

He knew the peasant's answer to the wish and gave it. "And you too."

The girl left the prison with a mist in her eyes. Her cousin looked at her with a queer, ironic little smile of affection. To be in trouble was a sure passport to the sympathy of Sheba. Now both her lovers were in a sad way. Diane wondered which of them would gain most from this new twist of fate.

Sheba turned to Mrs. Paget with an impulsive little burst of feminine ferocity. "Why do they put him in prison when they must know he didn't do it—that he couldn't do such a thing?"

"They don't all know as well as you do how noble he is, my dear," answered Diane dryly.

"But it's just absurd to think that he would plan

the murder of a man he has broken bread with for a few hundred dollars."

Diane flashed another odd little glance in the direction of her cousin. Probably Sheba was the one woman in Kusiak who did not know that Macdonald had served an ultimatum on Elliot to get out or fight and that their rivalry over her favor was at the bottom of the difficulty between them.

"It will work out all right," promised the older cousin.

Returning from their walk, they met Wally Selfridge coming out of the Paget house.

"Did you see Mr. Macdonald?" asked Diane.

"Yes. He's quite rational now." There was a jaunty little strut of triumph in Wally's cocksure manner.

Mrs. Paget knew he had made himself very busy securing evidence against Gordon. He was probably trying to curry favor with his chief. The little man always had been jealous of Peter. Perhaps he was attempting to rap him over the shoulder of Elliot because the Government official was a friend of Paget. Just now his insolent voice suggested a special cause for exultation.

The reason Wally was so pleased with himself was that he had dropped a hint into the ear of the wounded man not to clear Elliot of complicity in the attack upon him. The news that the special investigator had been arrested for robbery and attempted murder, flashed all over the United States, would go far to neutralize any report he might make against the validity of the Macdonald claims. If to this could be added later reports of an indictment, a trial, and possibly a conviction, it would not matter two straws what Elliot said in his official statement to the Land Office.

Since the attack upon his chief, Selfridge had moved on the presumption that Elliot had been in a conspiracy to get rid of him. He accepted the guilt of the field agent because this theory jumped with the interest of Wally and his friends. As a politician he intended to play this new development for all it was worth.

He had been shocked at the sight of Macdonald. The terrible beating and the loss of blood had sapped all the splendid, vital strength of the Scotchman. His battered head was swathed in bandages, but the white face was bruised and disfigured. The wounded man was weak as a kitten; only the steady eyes told that he was still strong and unconquered.

"I want to talk business for a minute, Miss Sedgwick. Will you please step out?" said Macdonald to his nurse.

She hesitated. "The doctor says—"

"Do as I say, please."

The nurse left them alone. Wally told the story of the evidence against Elliot in four sentences. His chief caught the point at once.

After Selfridge had gone, the wounded man lay silent thinking out his programme. Not for a moment did he doubt that he was going to live, and his brain was already busy planning for the future. By some freak of luck the cards had been stacked by destiny in his favor. He knew now that in the violence of his anger against Elliot he had made a mistake. To have killed his rival would have been fatal to the Kamatlah coal claims, would have alienated his best friends, and would have prejudiced hopelessly his chances with Sheba. Fate had been kind to him. He had been in the wrong and it had put him in the right. By the same cut of the cards young Elliot had been thrust down from an impregnable position to one in which he was a discredited suspect. With all this evidence to show that he had conspired against Macdonald, his report to the Department would be labor lost.

Diane came into the sick-room stripping her gloves after the walk. Macdonald smiled feebly at her and fired the first shot of his campaign to defeat the enemy.

"Has Elliot been captured yet?" he asked weakly.

The keen eyes of his hostess fastened upon him. "Captured! What do you mean? It was Gordon Elliot that brought you in and saved your life."

"Brought me from where?"

"From where he found you unconscious—at the ford."

"That's his story, is it?"

Macdonald shut his eyes wearily, but his incredulous voice had suggested a world of innuendo.

The young woman stood with her gloves crushed tight in both hands. It was her nature to be always a partisan. Without any reserve she was for Gordon in this new fight upon him. What had Wally Selfridge been saying to Macdonald? She longed mightily to ask the sick man some questions, but the orders of the doctor were explicit. Did the mine-owner mean to suggest that he had identified Elliot as one of his assailants? The thing was preposterous.

And yet—that was plainly what he had meant to imply. If he told such a story, things would go hard with Gordon. In court it would clinch the case against him by supplying the one missing link in the chain of circumstantial evidence.

Diane, in deep thought, frowned down upon the wounded man, who seemed already to have fallen into a light sleep. She told herself that this was some of Wally Selfridge's deviltry. Anyhow, she would talk it over with Peter.

CHAPTER XVIII
GORDON SPENDS
A BUSY EVENING

Paget smoked placidly, but the heart within him was troubled. It looked as if Selfridge had made up his mind to frame Gordon for a prison sentence. The worst of it was that he need not invent any evidence or take any chances. If Macdonald came through on the stand with an identification of Elliot as one of his assailants, the young man would go down the river to serve time. There was enough corroborative testimony to convict St. Peter himself.

It all rested with Macdonald—and the big Scotch-Canadian was a very uncertain quantity. His whole interests were at one in favor of getting Elliot out of the way. On the other hand—how far would he go to save the Kamatlah claims and to remove this good-looking rival from his path? Peter could not think he would stoop to perjury against an innocent man.

"I'm just telling you what he said," Diane explained. "And it worried me. His smile was cynical. I couldn't help thinking that if he wants to get even with Gordon—"

Mrs. Paget stopped. The maid had just brought

into the room a visitor. Diane moved forward and shook hands with him. "How do you do, Mr. Strong? Take this big chair."

Hanford Strong accepted the chair and a cigar. Though a well-to-do mine-owner, he wore as always the rough clothes of a prospector. He came promptly to the object of his call.

"I don't know whether this is where I should have come or not. Are you folks for young Elliot or are you for Selfridge?" he demanded.

"If you put it that way, we're for Elliot," smiled Peter.

"All right. Let me put it another way. You work for Mac. Are you on his side or on Elliot's in this matter of the coal claims?"

Diane looked at Peter. He took his time to answer.

"We hope the coal claimants will win, but we've got sense enough to see that Gordon is in here to report the facts. That's what he is paid for. He'll tell the truth as he sees it. If his superior officers decide on those facts against Macdonald, I don't see that Elliot is to blame."

"That's how it looks to me," agreed Strong. "I'm for a wide-open Alaska, but that don't make it right to put this young fellow through for a crime he didn't do. Lots of folks think he did it. That's all right. I know he didn't. Fact is, I like him. He's square. So I've come to tell you something."

206

He smoked for a minute silently before he continued.

"I've got no evidence in his favor, but I bumped into something a little while ago that didn't look good to me. You know I room next him at the hotel. I heard a noise in his room, and I thought that was funny, seeing as he was locked up in jail. So I kinder listened and heard whispers and the sound of some one moving about. There's a door between his room and mine that is kept locked. I looked through the keyhole, and in Elliot's room there was Wally Selfridge and another man. They were looking through papers at the desk. Wally put a stack of them in his pocket and they went out locking the door behind them."

"They had no business doing that," burst out Diane. "Wally Selfridge isn't an officer of the law."

Strong nodded dryly to her. "Just what I thought. So I followed them. They went to Macdonald's offices. After a while Wally came out and left the other man there. Then presently the lights went out. The man is camped there for the night. Will you tell me why?"

"Why?" repeated Diane with her sharp eyes on the miner.

"Because Wally has some papers there he don't want to get away from him."

"Some of Gordon's papers, of course."

"You've said it."

"All his notes and evidence in the case of the coal claims probably," contributed Peter.

"Maybe. Wally has stole them, but he hasn't nerve enough to burn them till he gets orders from Mac. So he's holding them safe at the office," guessed Strong.

"It's an outrage," Diane decided promptly.

"Surest thing you know. Wally has fixed it to frame him for prison and to play safe about his evidence on the coal claims."

"What are you going to do about it?" Diane asked her husband sharply.

Peter rose. "First I'm going to see Gordon and hear what he has to say. Come on, Strong. We may be gone quite a while, Diane. Don't wait up for me if you get through your stint of nursing."

Roused from sleep, Gopher Jones grumbled a good deal about letting the men see his prisoner. "You got all day, ain't you, without traipsing around here nights. Don't you figure I'm entitled to any rest?"

But he let them into the ramshackle building that served as a jail, and after three dollars had jingled in the palm of his hand he stepped outside and left the men alone with his prisoner. The three put their heads together and whispered.

"I'll meet you outside the house of Selfridge in half an hour, Strong," was the last thing that Gordon said before Jones came back to order out the visitors.

As soon as the place was dark again, Gordon set to work on the flimsy framework of his cell window. He knew already it was so decrepit that he could escape any time he desired, but until now there had been no reason why he should. Within a quarter of an hour he lifted the iron-grilled sash bodily from the frame and crawled through the window.

He found Paget and Strong waiting for him in the shadows of a pine outside the yard of Selfridge.

"To begin with, you walk straight home and go to bed, Peter," the young man announced. "You're not in this. You're not invited to our party. I don't have to tell you why, do I?"

The engineer understood the reason. He was an employee of Macdonald, a man thoroughly trusted by him. Even though Gordon intended only to right a wrong, it was better that Paget should not be a party to it. Reluctantly Peter went home.

Gordon turned to Strong. "I owe you a lot already. There's no need for you to run a risk of getting into trouble for me. If things break right, I can do what I have to do without help."

"And if they don't?" Strong waved an impatient hand. "Cut it out, Elliot. I've taken a fancy to go through with this. I never did like Selfridge any-how, and I ain't got a wife and I don't work for Mac. Why the hell shouldn't I have some fun?"

Gordon shrugged his shoulders. "All right. Might as well play ball and get things moving, then."

The little miner knocked at the door. Wally himself opened. Elliot, from the shelter of the pine, saw the two men in talk. Selfridge shut the door and came to the edge of the porch. He gave a gasp and his hands went trembling into the air. The six-gun of the miner had been pressed hard against his fat paunch. Under curt orders he moved down the steps and out of the yard to the tree.

At sight of Gordon the eyes of Wally stood out in amazement. Little sweat beads burst out on his forehead, for he remembered how busy he had been collecting evidence against this man.

"W-w-what do you want?" he asked.

"Got your keys with you?"

"Y-yes."

"Come with us."

Wally breathed more freely. For a moment he had thought this man had come to take summary vengeance on him.

They led him by alleys and back streets to the office of the Macdonald Yukon Trading Company. Under orders he knocked on the door and called out who he was. Gordon crouched close to the log wall, Strong behind him.

"Let me in, Olson," ordered Selfridge again.

The door opened, and a man stood on the

threshold. Elliot was on top of him like a panther. The man went down as though his knees were oiled hinges. Before he could gather his slow wits, the barrel of a revolver was shoved against his teeth.

"Take it easy, Olson," advised Gordon. "Get up—slowly. Now, step back into the office. Keep your hands up."

Strong closed and locked the door behind them.

"I want my papers, Selfridge. Dig up your keys and get them for me," Elliot commanded.

Wally did not need any keys. He knew the combination of the safe and opened it. From an inner drawer he drew a bunch of papers. Gordon looked them over carefully. Strong sat on a table and toyed with a revolver which he jammed playfully into the stomach of his fat prisoner.

"All here," announced the field agent.

The safe-robbers locked their prisoners in the office and disappeared into the night. They stopped at the house of the collector of customs, a genial young fellow with whom Elliot had played tennis a good deal, and left the papers in his hands for safe-keeping. After which they returned to the hotel and reached the second floor by way of the back stairs used by the servants.

Here they parted, each going to his own room. Gordon slept like a schoolboy and woke only when the sun poured through the window upon his bed in a broad ribbon of warm gold.

He got up, bathed, dressed, and went down into the hotel dining-room. The waiters looked at him in amazement. Presently the cook peered in at him from the kitchen and the clerk made an excuse to drop into the room. Gordon ate as if nothing were the matter, apparently unaware of the excitement he was causing. He paid not the least attention to the nudging and the whispering. After he had finished breakfast, he lit a cigar, leaned back in his chair, and smoked placidly.

Presently an eruption of men poured into the room. At the head of them was Gopher Jones. Near the rear Wally Selfridge lingered modestly. He was not looking for hazardous adventure.

"Whad you doing here?" demanded Gopher, bristling up to Elliot.

The young man watched a smoke wreath float ceilingward before he turned his mild gaze on the chief of police.

"I'm smoking."

"Don't you know we just got in from hunting you—two posses of us been out all night?" Gopher glared savagely at the smoker.

Gordon looked distressed. "That's too bad. There's a telephone in my room, too. Why didn't you call up? I've been there all night."

"The deuce you have," exploded Jones. "And us combing the hills for you. Young man, you're mighty smart. But I want to tell you that you'll pay for this."

"Did you want me for anything in particular— or just to get up a poker game?" asked Elliot suavely.

The leader of the posse gave himself to a job of scientific profanity. He was spurred on to outdo himself because he had heard a titter or two behind him. When he had finished, he formed a procession. He, with Elliot handcuffed beside him, was at the head of it. It marched to the jail.

CHAPTER XIX
SHEBA DOES NOT THINK SO

The fingers of Sheba were busy with the embroidery upon which she worked, but her thoughts were full of the man who lay asleep on the lounge. His strong body lay at ease, relaxed.

Already health was flowing back into his veins. Beneath the tan of the lean, muscular cheeks a warmer color was beginning to creep. Soon he would be about again, vigorous and forceful, striding over obstacles to the goal he had set himself.

Just now she was the chief goal of his desire. Sheba did not deceive herself into thinking that he had for a moment accepted her dismissal of him.

He still meant to marry her, and he had told her so in characteristic way the day after their break.

Sheba had sent him a check for the amount he had paid her and had refused to see him or anybody else.

Shamed and humiliated, she had kept to her room. The check had come back to her by mail.

Across the face of it he had written in his strong handwriting:—

I don't welsh on my bets. You can't give to me what is not mine.

Do not think for an instant that I shall not marry you.

Watching him now, she wondered what manner of man he was. There had been a day or two when she had thought she understood him. Then she had learned, from the story of Meteetse, how far his world of thought was from hers. That which to her had put a gulf between them was to him only an incident.

She moved to adjust a window blind and when she returned found that his steady eyes were fixed upon her.

"You're getting better fast," she said.

"Yes."

The girl had a favor to ask of him and lest her courage fail she plunged into it.

"Mr. Macdonald, if you say the word Mr. Elliot will be released on bail. I am thinking you will be so good as to say it."

His narrowed eyes held a cold glitter. "Why?"

"You must know he is innocent. You must—"

"I know only what the evidence shows," he cut in, warily on his guard. "He may or may not have been one of my attackers. From the first blow I was dazed. But everything points to it that he hired—"

216

"Oh, no!" interrupted the Irish girl, her dark eyes shining softly. "The way of it is that he saved your life, that he fought for you, and that he is in prison because of it."

"If that is true, why doesn't he bring some proof of it?"

"Proof!" she cried scornfully. "Between friends—"

"He's no friend of mine. The man is a meddler. I despise him."

The scarlet flooded her cheeks. "And I am liking him very, very much," she flung back stanchly.

Macdonald looked up at the vivid, flushed face and found it wholly charming. He liked her none the less because her fine eyes were hot and defiant in behalf of his rival.

"Very well," he smiled. "I'll get him out if you'll do me a good turn too."

"Thank you. It's a bargain."

"Then sing to me."

She moved to the piano "What shall I sing?"

"Sing 'Divided.' "

The long lashes veiled her soft eyes while she considered. In a way he had tricked her into singing for him a love-song she did not want to sing. But she made no protest. Swiftly she turned and slid along the bench. Her fingers touched the keys and she began.

He watched the beauty and warmth of her

dainty youth with eyes that mirrored the hunger of his heart. How buoyantly she carried her dusky little head! With what a gallant spirit she did all things! He was usually a frank pagan, but when he was with her it seemed to him that God spoke through her personality all sorts of brave, fine promises.

Sheba paid her pledge in full. After the first two stanzas were finished she sang the last ones as well:—

"An' what about the wather when
    I'd have ould Paddy's boat,
Is it me that would be feared to
    grip the oars an' go afloat?
Oh, I could find him by the light
    of sun or moon or star:
But there's caulder things than salt waves
    between us, so they are.
            Och anee!

"Sure well I know he'll never have
    the heart to come to me,
An' love is wild as any wave
    that wanders on the sea,
'T is the same if he is near me,
't is the same if he is far:
His thoughts are hard an' ever hard
    between us, so they are.
            Och anee!"

Her hands dropped from the keys and she turned slowly on the end of the seat. The dark lashes fell to her hot cheeks. He did not speak, but she felt the steady insistence of his gaze. In self-defense she looked at him.

The pallor of his face lent accent to the fire that smouldered in his eyes.

"I'm going to marry you, Sheba. Make up your mind to that, girl," he said harshly.

There was infinite pity in the look she gave him. " 'There's caulder things than salt waves between us, so they are,' " she quoted.

"Not if I love you and you love me. By God, I trample down everything that comes between us."

He swung to a sitting position on the lounge. Through the steel-gray eyes in the brooding face his masterful spirit wrestled with hers. A lean-loined Samson, with broad, powerful shoulders and deep chest, he dominated his world ruthlessly. But this slim Irish girl with the young, lissom body held her own.

"Must we go through that again?" she asked gently.

"Again and again until you see reason."

She knew the tremendous driving power of the man and she was afraid in her heart that he would sweep her from the moorings to which she clung.

"There is something else I haven't told you." The embarrassed lashes lifted bravely from the flushed cheeks to meet steadily his look. "I don't think—that I—care for you. 'T is I that am shamed at my—fickleness. But I don't—not with the full of my heart."

His bold, possessive eyes yielded no fraction of all they claimed. "Time enough for that, Sheba. Truth is that you're afraid to let yourself love me. You're worried because you can't measure me by the little two-by-four foot-rule you brought from Ireland with you."

Sheba nodded her dusky little head in naive candor. "I think there will be some truth in that, Mr. Macdonald. You're lawless, you know."

"I'm a law to myself, if that's what you mean. It is my business to help hammer out an empire in this Northland. If I let my work be cluttered up by all the little rules made by little men for other little ones, my plans would come to a standstill. I am a practical man, but I keep sight of the vision. No need for me to brag. What I have done speaks for me as a guidepost to what I mean to do."

"I know," the girl admitted with the impetuous generosity of her race. "I hear it from everybody. You have built towns and railroads and developed mines and carried the twentieth century into new outposts. You have given work to thousands. But you go so fast I can't keep step with you. I am one of the little folks for whom laws were made."

"Then I'll make a new code for you," he said,

smiling. "Just do as I say and everything will come out right."

Faintly her smile met his. "My grandmother might have agreed to that. But we live in a new world for women. They have to make their own decisions. I suppose that is a part of the penalty we pay for freedom."

Diane came into the room and Macdonald turned to her.

"I have just been telling Sheba that I am going to marry her—that there is no escape for her. She had better get used to the idea that I intend to make her happy."

The older cousin glanced at Sheba and laughed with a touch of embarrassment. "Whether she wants to be happy or not, O Cave Man?"

"I'm going to make her want to."

Sheba fled, but from the door she flung back her challenge. "I don't think so."

CHAPTER XX
GORDON FINDS HIMSELF UNPOPULAR

Macdonald kept his word to Sheba. He used his influence to get Elliot released, and with a touch of cynicism quite characteristic went on the bond of his rival. An information was filed against the field agent of the Land Department for highway robbery and attempted murder, but Gordon went about his business just as if he were not under a cloud.

None the less, he walked the streets a marked man. Women and children looked at him curiously and whispered as he passed. The sullen, hostile eyes of miners measured him silently. He was aware that feeling had focused against him with surprising intensity of resentment, and he suspected that the whispers of Wally Selfridge were largely responsible for this.

For Wally saw to it that in the minds of the miners Elliot in his own person stood for the enemies of the open-Alaska policy. He scattered broadcast garbled extracts from the first preliminary report of the field agent, and in the coal camps he spread the impression that the whole mining activities of the Territory would be curtailed if Elliot had his way.

223

In the States the fight between the coal claimants and their foes was growing more bitter. The muckrakers were busy, and the sentiment outside had settled so definitely against granting the patents that the National Administration might at any time jettison Macdonald and his backers as a sop to public opinion.

It was not hard for Gordon to guess how unpopular he was, but he did not let this interfere with his activities. He moved to and fro among the mining camps with absolute disregard of the growing hatred against him.

Paget came to him at last with a warning.

"What's this I hear about you being almost killed up on Bonanza?" Peter wanted to know.

"Down in the None Such Mine, you mean? It did seem to be raining hammers as I went down the shaft," admitted his friend.

"Were the hammers dropped on purpose?"

Gordon looked at him with a grim smile. "Your guess is just as good as mine, Peter. What do you think?"

Peter answered seriously. "I think it isn't safe for you to take the chances you do, Gordon. I find a wrong impression about you prevalent among the men. They are blaming you for stirring up all this trouble on the outside, and they are worried for fear the mines may close and they will lose their jobs. I tell you that they are in a dangerous mood."

"Sorry, but I can't help that."

"You can stay around town and not go out alone nights, can't you?"

"I dare say I can, but I'm not going to."

"Some of these men are violent. They don't think straight about you—"

"Kindness of Mr. Selfridge," contributed Gordon.

"Perhaps. Anyhow, there's a lot of sullen hate brewing against you. Don't invite an explosion. That would be just kid foolhardiness."

"You think I'd better buy another automatic gat," said Elliot with a grin.

"I think you had better use a little sense, Gordon. I dare say I am exaggerating the danger. But when you go around with that jaunty, devil-may-care way of yours, the men think you are looking for trouble—and you're likely to get it."

"Am I?"

"I know what I'm talking about. Nine out of ten of the men think you tried to murder Macdonald after you had robbed him and that your nerve weakened on the job. This seems to some of the most lawless to give them a moral right to put you out of the way. Anyhow, it is a kind of justification, according to their point of view. I'm not defending it, of course. I'm telling you so that you can appreciate your danger."

"You have done your duty, then, Peter."

"But you don't intend to take my advice?"

225

"I'll tell you what I told you last time when you warned me. I'm going through with the job I've been hired to do, just as you would stick it out in my place. I don't think I'm in much danger. Men in general are law-abiding. They growl, but they don't go as far as murder."

Peter gave him up. After all, the chances were that Gordon was right. Alaska was not a lawless country. And it might be that the best way to escape peril was to walk through it with a grin as if it did not exist.

The next issue of the Kusiak "Sun" contained a bitter editorial attack upon Elliot. The occasion for it was a press dispatch from Washington to the effect that the pressure of public opinion had become so strong that Winton, Commissioner of the General Land Office, might be forced to resign his place. This was a blow to the coal claimants, and the "Sun" charged in vitriolic language that the reports of Elliot were to blame. He was, the newspaper claimed, an enemy to all those who had come to Alaska to earn an honest living there. Under indictment for attempted murder and for highway robbery, this man was not satisfied with having tried to kill from ambush the best friend Alaska had ever known. In every report that he sent to Washington he was dealing underhanded blows at the prosperity of Alaska. He was a snake in the grass, and as such every decent man ought to hold him in scorn.

Elliot read this just as he was leaving for the Willow Creek Camp. He thrust the paper impatiently into his coat pocket and swung to the saddle. Why did they persecute him? He had told nothing but the truth, nothing not required of him by the simplest, elemental honesty. Yet he was treated as an outcast and a criminal. The injustice of it was beginning to rankle.

He was temperamentally an optimist, but depression rode with him to the gold camp and did not lift from his spirits till he started back next day for Kusiak. The news had been flashed by wire all over the United States that he was a crook. His friends and relatives could give no adequate answer to the fact that an indictment hung over his head. In Alaska he was already convicted by public opinion. Even the Pagets were lined up as to their interests with Macdonald. Sheba liked him and believed in him. Her loyal heart acquitted him of all blame. But it was to the wooing of his enemy that she had listened rather than to his. The big Scotchman had run against a barrier, but his rival expected him to trample it down. He would wear away the scruples of Sheba by the pressure of his masterful will.

In the late afternoon, while Gordon was still fifteen miles from Kusiak, his horse fell lame. He led it limping to the cabin of some miners.

There were three of them, and they had been

drinking heavily from a jug of whiskey left earlier in the day by the stage-driver. Gordon was in two minds whether to accept their surly permission to stay for the night, but the lameness of his horse decided him.

Not caring to invite their hostility, he gave his name as Gordon instead of Elliot. He was to learn within the hour that this was mistake number two.

From a pocket of the coat he had thrown on a bed protruded the newspaper Gordon had brought from Kusiak. One of the men, a big red-headed fellow, pulled it out and began sulkily to read.

While he read the other two bickered and drank and snarled at each other. All three of the men were in that stage of drunkenness when a quarrel is likely to flare up at a moment's notice.

"Listen here," demanded the man with the newspaper. "Tell you what, boys, I'm going to wring the neck of that pussyfooting spy Elliot if I ever get a chanct."

He read aloud the editorial in the "Sun." After he had finished, the others joined him in a chorus of curses.

"I always did hate a spy—and this one's a murderer too. Why don't some one fill his hide with lead?" one of the men wanted to know.

Redhead was sitting at the table. He thumped a heavy fist down so hard that the tin cups jumped.

"Gimme a crack at him and I'll show you, by God."

A shadow fell across the room. In the doorway stood a newcomer. Gordon had a sensation as if a lump of ice had been drawn down his spine. For the man who had just come in was Big Bill Macy, and he was looking at the field agent with eyes in which amazement, anger, and triumph blazed.

"I'm glad to death to meet up with you again, Mr. Elliot," he jeered. "Seems like old times on Wild-Goose."

"Whad you say his name is?" cut in the man with the newspaper.

"Hasn't he introduced himself, boys?" Macy answered with a cruel grin. "Now, ain't that modest of him? You lads are entertaining that well-known deteckative and spy Gordon Elliot, that renowned king of hold-ups—"

The red-headed man interrupted with a howl of rage. "If you're telling it straight, Bill Macy, I'll learn him to spy on me?"

Elliot was sitting on one of the beds. He had not moved an inch since Macy had appeared, but the brain behind his live eyes was taking stock of the situation. Big Bill blocked the doorway. The table was in front of the window. Unless he could fight his way out, there was no escape for him. He was trapped.

Quietly Gordon looked from one to another. He read no hope in the eyes of any.

"I'm not spying on you. My horse is lame. You can see that for yourself. All I asked was a night's lodging."

"Under another name than your own, you damned sneak."

The field agent did not understand the fury of the man, because he did not know that these miners were working the claim under a defective title and that they had jumped to the conclusion that he had come to get evidence against them. But he knew that never in his life had he been in a tighter hole. In another minute they would attack him. Whether it would run to murder he could not tell. At the best he would be hammered helpless.

But no evidence of this knowledge appeared in his manner.

"I didn't give my last name because there is a prejudice against me in this country," he explained in an even voice.

He wondered as he spoke if he had better try to fling himself through the window sash. There might be a remote chance that he could make it.

The miner at the table killed this possibility by rising and standing squarely in the road.

"Look out! He's got a gat," warned Macy.

Gordon fervently wished he had. But he was unarmed. While his eyes quested for a weapon he played for time.

"You can't get away with this, you know. The

230

United States Government is back of me. It's known I left the Willow Creek Camp. I'll be traced here."

Through Gordon's mind there flashed a word of advice once given him by a professional prize-fighter: "If you get in a rough house, don't wait for the other fellow to hit first."

They were crouching for the attack. In another moment they would be upon him. Almost with one motion he stooped, snatched up by the leg a heavy stool, and sprang to the bed upon which he had been sitting.

The four men closed with him in a rush. They came at him low, their heads protected by uplifted arms. His memory brought to him a picture of the whitewashed gridiron of a football field, and in it he saw a vision of safety.

The stool crashed down upon Big Bill Macy's head. Gordon hurdled the crumpling figure, plunged between hands outstretched to seize him, and over the table went through the window, taking the flimsy sash with him.

CHAPTER XXI
A NEW WAY OF
LEAVING A HOUSE

The surge of disgust with which Sheba had broken her engagement to marry Macdonald ebbed away as the weeks passed. It was impossible for her to wait upon him in his illness and hold any repugnance toward this big, elemental man. The thing he had done might be wrong, but the very openness and frankness of his relation to Meteetse redeemed it from shame. He was neither a profligate nor a squawman.

This was Diane's point of view, and in time it became to a certain extent that of Sheba. One takes on the color of one's environment, and the girl from Drogheda knew in her heart that Meteetse and Colmac were no longer the real barriers that stood between her and the Alaskan. She had been disillusioned, saw him more clearly; and though she still recognized the quality of bigness that set him apart, her spirit did not now do such complete homage to it. More and more her thoughts contrasted him with another man.

Macdonald did not need to be told that he had lost ground, but with the dogged determination that had carried him to success he refused to

233

accept the verdict. She was a woman, therefore to be won. The habit of victory was so strong in him that he could see no alternative.

He embarrassed her with his downright attentions, hemmed her in with courtesies she could not evade. If she appealed to her cousin, Diane only laughed.

"My dear, you might as well make up your mind to him. He is going to marry you, willy-nilly."

Sheba herself began to be afraid he would. There was something dominant and masterful about the man that swept opposition aside. He had a way of getting what he wanted.

The motor-car picnic to the Willow Creek Camp was a case in point. Sheba did not want to go, but she went. She would much rather have sat in the rear seat with Diane,—at least, she persuaded herself that she would,—yet she occupied the place beside Macdonald in front. The girl was a rebel. Still, in her heart, she was not wholly reluctant. He made a strong appeal to her imagination. She felt that it would have been impossible for any girl to be indifferent to the wooing of such a man.

The picnic was a success. Macdonald was an outdoor man rather than a parlor one. He took charge of the luncheon, lit the fire, and cooked the coffee without the least waste of effort. In his shirt-sleeves, the neck open at the throat, he looked the embodiment of masculine vigor. Diane could not help mentioning it to her cousin.

"Isn't he a splendid human animal?"

Sheba nodded. "He's wonderful."

"If I were a little Irish colleen and he had done me the honor to care for me, I'd have fallen fathoms deep in love with him."

The Irish colleen's eyes grew reflective. "Not if you had seen Peter first, Di. There's nothing reasonable about a girl, I do believe. She loves— or else she just doesn't."

Diane fired a question at her point-blank. "Have you met *your* Peter? Is that why you hang back?"

The color flamed into Sheba's face. "Of course not. You do say the most outrageous things, Di."

They had driven to Willow Creek over the river road. They returned by way of the hills. Macdonald drew up in front of a cabin to fill the radiator.

He stood listening beside the car, the water bucket in his hand. Something unusual was going on inside the house. There came the sound of a thud, of a groan, and then the crash of breaking glass. The whole window frame seemed to leap from the side of the house. The head and shoulders of a man projected through the broken glass.

The man swept himself free of the débris and started to run. Instantly he pulled up in his stride, as amazed to see those in the car as they were to see him.

"Gordon!" cried Diane.

Out of the house poured a rush of men. They too pulled up abruptly at sight of Macdonald and his guests.

A sardonic mirth gleamed in the eyes of the Scotchman. "Do you always come out of a house through the wall, Mr. Elliot?" he asked.

"Only when I'm in a hurry." Gordon pulled out a handkerchief and dabbed at some glass cuts on his face.

"Don't let us detain you," said the Alaskan satirically. "We'll excuse you, since you must go."

"I'm not in such a hurry now. In fact, if you're going to Kusiak, I think I'll ask you for a lift," returned the field agent coolly.

"And your friends-in-a-hurry—do they want a lift too?"

Big Bill Macy came swaying forward, both hands to his bleeding head. "He's a spy, curse him. And he tried to kill me."

"Did he?" commented Macdonald evenly. "What were you doing to him?"

"He can't sneak around our claim under a false name," growled one of the miners. "We'll beat his damn head off."

"I've had notions like that myself sometimes," assented the big Scotchman. "But I think we had

236

all better leave Mr. Elliot to the law. He has Uncle Sam back of him in his spying, and none of us are big enough to buck the Government." Crisply Macdonald spoke to Gordon, turning upon him cold, hostile eyes. "Get in if you're going to."

Elliot met him eye to eye. "I've changed my mind. I'm going to walk."

"That's up to you."

Gordon shook hands with Diane and Sheba, went into the house for his coat, and walked to the stable. He brought out his horse and turned it loose, then took the road himself for Kusiak.

A couple of miles out the car passed him trudging townward. As they flashed down the road he waved a cheerful and nonchalant greeting.

Sheba had been full of gayety and life, but her mood was changed. All the way home she was strangely silent.

CHAPTER XXII
GID HOLT COMES TO KUSIAK

The days grew short. In sporting circles the talk was no longer of the midnight Fourth of July baseball game, but of preparation for the Alaska Sweepstakes, since the shadow of the cold Arctic winter had crept down to the Yukon and touched its waters to stillness. Men, gathered around warm stoves, spoke of the merits of huskies and Siberian wolf-hounds, of the heavy fall of snow in the hills, of the overhauling of outfits and the transportation of supplies to distant camps.

The last river boat before the freeze-up had long since gone. A month earlier the same steamer had taken down in a mail sack the preliminary report of Elliot to his department chief. One of the passengers on that trip had been Selfridge, sent out to counteract the influence of the evidence against the claimants submitted by the field agent. An information had been filed against Gordon for highway robbery and attempted murder. Wally was to see that the damning facts against him were brought to the attention of officials in high places where the charges would do most good. The details of the story were to be held in reserve for publicity in case the muckrake magazines should try to make capital of the report of Elliot.

Kusiak found much time for gossip during the long nights. It knew that Macdonald had gone on the bond of Elliot in spite of the scornful protest of the younger man. The two gave each other chilly nods of greeting when they met, but friends were careful not to invite them to the same social affairs. The case against the field agent was pending. Pursuit of the miners who had robbed the big mine-owner had long ago been dropped. Somewhere in the North the outlaws lay hidden, swallowed up by the great white waste of snow.

The general opinion was that Mac was playing politics about the trial of his rival. He would not let the case come to a jury until the time when a conviction would have most effect in the States, the gossips predicted. They did not know that he was waiting for the return of Wally Selfridge.

The whispers touched closely the personal affairs of Macdonald. The report of his engagement to Sheba O'Neill had been denied, but it was noticed that he was a constant guest at the home of the Pagets. Young Elliot called there too. Almost any day one or other of the two men could be seen with Sheba on the street. Those who wanted to take a sporting chance on the issue knew that odds were offered *sub rosa* at the Pay Streak saloon of three to one on Mac.

As for Sheba, she rebelled impotently at the situation. The mine-owner would not take "No" for an answer. He wooed her with a steady, dominant persistence that shook even her strong, young will. There was something resistless in the way he took her for granted. Gordon Elliot had not mentioned love to her, though there were times when her heart fluttered for fear he would. She did not want any more complications. She wanted to be let alone. So when an invitation came from her little friends the Husteds, signed by all three of the children, asking her to come and visit them at the camp back of Katma, the Irish girl jumped at the chance to escape for a time from the decision being forced upon her.

Sheba pledged her cousin to secrecy until after she had gone, so that Miss O'Neill was able to slip away on the stage unnoticed either by Macdonald or Elliot. The only other passenger was an elderly woman going up to the Katma camp to take a place as cook.

Later on the same day Wally Selfridge, coming in over the ice, reached Kusiak with important news for his chief. He brought with him an order from Winton, Commissioner of the General Land Office, suspending Elliot pending an investigation of the charges against him. The field agent was to forward by mail all documents in his possession and for the time, at least, drop the matter of the coal claims.

Oddly enough, it was to Genevieve Mallory that Macdonald went for consolation when he learned that Sheba had left town. He had always found it very pleasant to drop in for a chat with her, and she saw to it that he met the same friendly welcome now that a rival had annexed his scalp to her slender waist. For Mrs. Mallory did not concede defeat. If the Irish girl could be eliminated, she believed she would yet win.

His hostess laced her fingers behind her beautiful, tawny head, quite well aware that the attitude set off the perfect modeling of the soft, supple body. She looked up at him with a mocking little smile.

"Rumor says that she has run away, my lord. Is it true?"

"Yes. Slipped away on the stage this morning."

"That's a good sign. She was afraid to stay."

It was a part of the fiction between them that Mrs. Mallory was to give him the benefit of her advice in his wooing of her rival. She seemed to take it for granted that he would at last marry Sheba after wearing away the rigid Puritanism of her resentment.

Macdonald had never liked her so well as now. Her point of view was so sane, so reasonable. It asked for no impossible virtues in a man. There was something restful in her genial, derisive understanding of him. She had a silent divination of his moods and ministered indolently to them.

"Do you think so? Ought I to follow her?" he asked.

She showed a row of perfect teeth in a low ripple of amusement. The situation at least was piquant, even though it was at her expense.

"No. Give the girl time. Catch her impulse on the rebound. She'll be bored to death at Katma and she will come back docile."

Her scarlet lips, the long, unbroken lines of the sinuous, opulent body, the challenge of the smouldering eyes, the warmth of her laughter, all invited him to forget the charms of other women. The faint feminine perfume of her was wafted to his brain. He felt a besieging of the blood.

Stepping behind the chair in which she sat, he tilted back the head of lustrous bronze, and very deliberately kissed her on the lips.

For a moment she gave herself to his embrace, then pushed him back, rose, and walked across the room to a little table. With fingers that trembled slightly she lit a cigarette. Sheathed in her close-fitting gown, she made a strong carnal appeal to him, but there was between them, too, a close bond of the spirit. He made no apologies, no explanation.

Presently she turned and looked at him. Only the deeper color beneath her eyes betrayed any excitement.

"Unless I'm a bad prophet you'll get the answer you want when she comes back, Colby."

He thought her reply to his indiscretion superb. It admitted complicity, reproached, warned, and at the same time ignored. Never before had she called him by his given name. He took it as a token of forgiveness and renunciation.

Why was it not Genevieve Mallory that he wanted to marry? It would be the wise thing to do. She would ask nothing of him that he could not give, and she would bring to him many things that he wanted. But he was under the spell of Sheba's innocence, of the mystery of her youth, of the charm she had brought with her from the land of fairies and banshees. The reasonable course made just now not enough appeal to him. He craved the rapture of an impossible adventure into a world wonderful.

The mine-owner carried with him back to his office a sense of the futile irony of life. A score of men would have liked to marry Mrs. Mallory. She had all the sophisticated graces of life and much of the natural charm of an unusually attractive personality. He had only to speak the word to win her, and his fancy had flown in pursuit of a little Puritan with no knowledge of the world.

In front of the Seattle & Kusiak Emporium the Scotchman stopped. A little man who had his back to him was bargaining for a team of huskies. The man turned, and Macdonald recognized him.

"Hello, Gid. Aren't you off your usual beat a bit?" he asked.

The little miner looked him over impudently. "Well—well! If it ain't the Big Mogul himself—

and wantin' to know if I've got permission to travel off the reservation."

Macdonald laughed tolerantly. He had that large poise which is not disturbed by the sand stings of life.

"I reckon you travel where you want to, Gid,— same as I do."

"Maybeso. I shouldn't wonder if you'd find out quite soon enough what I'm doing here. You never can tell," the old man retorted with a manner that concealed volumes.

Those who were present remembered the words and in the light of what took place later thought them significant.

"Anyhow, it is quite a social event for Kusiak," Macdonald suggested with a smile of irony.

Without more words Holt turned back to his bargaining. The big Scotchman went on his way, remembered that he wanted to see the cashier of the bank which he controlled, and promptly forgot that old Gid existed.

The old man concluded his purchase and drove up to the hotel behind one of the best dog teams in Alaska. He had paid one hundred dollars down and was to settle the balance next day.

Gideon asked a question of the porter.

"Second floor. That's his room up there," the man answered, pointing to a window.

"Oh, you, seven—eighteen—ninety-nine," the little miner shouted up.

Elliot appeared at the window. "Well, I'll be hanged! What are you doing here, Old-Timer?"

"Onct I knew a man lived to be a grandpa minding his own business," grinned the little man. "Come down and I'll tell you all about it, boy."

In half a minute Gordon was beside him. After the first greetings the young man nodded toward the dog team.

"How did you persuade Tim Ryan to lend you his huskies?"

"Why don't you take a paper and keep up with the news, son? These huskies don't belong to Tim."

"Meaning that Mr. Gideon Holt is the owner?"

"You've done guessed it," admitted the miner complacently.

He had a right to be proud of the team. It was a famous one even in the North. It had run second for two years in the Alaska Sweepstakes to Macdonald's great Siberian wolf-hounds. The leader Butch was the hero of a dozen races and a hundred savage fights.

"What in Halifax do you want with the team?" asked Elliot, surprised. "The whole outfit must have cost a small fortune."

"Some dust," admitted Gideon proudly. He winked mysteriously at Gordon. "I got a use for this team, if any one was to ask you."

"Haven't taken the Government mail contract, have you?"

"Not so you could notice it. I'll tell you what I want with this team, as the old sayin' is." Holt lowered his voice and narrowed slyly his little beadlike eyes. "I'm going to put a crimp in Colby Macdonald. That's what I aim to do with it."

"How?"

The miner beckoned Elliot closer and whispered in his ear.

CHAPTER XXIII
IN THE DEAD OF NIGHT

While Kusiak slept that night the wind shifted. It came roaring across the range and drove before it great scudding clouds heavily-laden with sleety snow. The howling storm snuffed out the moonlight as if it had been a tallow dip and fought and screamed around the peaks, whirling down the gulches with the fury of a blizzard.

From dark till dawn the roar of the wind filled the night. Before morning heavy drifts had wiped out the roads and sheeted the town in virgin white unbroken by trails or furrows.

With the coming of daylight the tempest abated. Kusiak got into its working clothes and dug itself out from the heavy blanket of white that had tucked it in. By noon the business of the town was under way again. That which would have demoralized the activities of a Southern city made little difference to these Arctic Circle dwellers. Roads were cleared, paths shoveled, stores opened. Children in parkas and fur coats trooped to school and studied through the short afternoon by the aid of electric light.

Dusk fell early and with it came a scatter of more snow. Mrs. Selfridge gave a dinner-dance at the club that night and her guests came in furs of great variety and much value. The hostess outdid herself to make the affair the most elaborate of the season. Wally had brought the favors in from Seattle and also the wines. Nobody in Kusiak of any social importance was omitted from the list of invited except Gordon Elliot. Even the grumpy old cashier of Macdonald's bank—an old bachelor who lived by himself in rooms behind those in which the banking was done—was persuaded to break his custom and appear in a rusty old dress suit of the vintage of '95.

The grizzled cashier—his name was Robert Milton—left the clubhouse early for his rooms. It was snowing, but the wind had died down. Contrary to his custom, he had taken two or three glasses of wine. His brain was excited so that he knew he could not sleep. He decided to read "Don Quixote" by the stove for an hour or two. The heat and the reading together would make him drowsy.

Arrived at the bank, he let himself into his rooms and locked the door. He stooped to open the draft of the stove when a sound stopped him halfway. The cashier stood rigid, still crouched, waiting for a repetition of the noise. It came once more—the low, dull rasping of a file.

Shivers ran down the spine of Milton and up the back of his head to the roots of his hair. Somebody was in the bank—at two o'clock in the morning—with tools for burglary. He was a scholarly old fellow, brought up in New England and cast out to the uttermost frontier by the malign tragedy of poverty. Adventure offered no appeal to him. His soul quaked as he waited with slack, feeble muscles upon the discovery that only a locked door stood between him and violent ruffians.

But though his knees trembled beneath him and the sickness of fear was gripping his heart, Robert Milton had in him the dynamic spark that makes a man. He tiptoed to his desk and with shaking fingers gripped the revolver that lay in a drawer.

The cashier stood there for a moment, moistening his dry lips with his tongue and trying to swallow the lump that rose to his throat and threatened to stop his breathing. He braced himself for the plunge, then slowly trod across the room to the inner, locked door. The palsied fingers of his left hand could scarce turn the key.

It seemed to him that the night was alive with the noise he made in turning the lock and opening the door. The hinges grated and the floor squeaked beneath the fall of his foot as he stood at the threshold.

Two men were in front of the wire grating which protected the big safe that filled the alcove to the right. One held a file and the other a candle. Their blank, masked faces were turned toward Milton, and each of them covered him with a weapon.

"W-what are you doing here?" quavered the cashier.

"Drop that gun," came the low, sharp command from one of them.

Under the menace of their revolvers the heart of Milton pumped water instead of blood. The strength oozed out of him. His body swayed and he shut his eyes. A hand groped for the casement of the door to steady him.

"Drop it—quick."

Some old ancestral instinct in the bank cashier rose out of his panic to destroy him. He wanted to lie down quietly in a faint. But his mind asserted its mastery over the weakling body. In spite of his terror, of his flaccid will, he had to keep the faith. He was guardian of the bank funds. At all costs he must protect them.

His forearm came up with a jerk. Two shots rang out almost together. The cashier sagged back against the wall and slowly slid to the floor.

The guests of Mrs. Selfridge danced well into the small hours. The California champagne that Wally had brought in stimulated a gayety that was balm to his wife's soul. She wanted her dinner-dance to be smart, to have the atmosphere she had found in the New York cabarets. If every-body talked at once, she felt they were having a good time. If nobody listened to anybody else, it proved that the affair was a screaming success.

Mrs. Wally was satisfied as she bade her guests good-bye and saw them pass into the heavy snow that was again falling. They all assured her that there had not been so hilarious a party in Kusiak. One old-timer, a trifle lit up by reason of too much hospitality, phrased his enjoyment a little awkwardly.

"It's been great, Mrs. Selfridge. Nothing like it since the days of the open dance hall."

Mrs. Mallory hastily suppressed an internal smile and stepped into the breach. "*How* do you do it?" she asked her hostess enviously.

"My dear, if *you* say it was a success—"

"What else could one say?"

Genevieve Mallory always preferred to tell the truth when it would do just as well. Now it did better, since it contributed to her own ironic sense of amusement. Macdonald had once told her that Mrs. Selfridge made him think of the saying, "Monkey sees, monkey does." The effervescent little woman had never had an original idea in her life.

Most of those who had been at the dance slept late. They were oblivious of the fact that the storm had quickened again into a howling gale. Nor did they know the two bits of news that were passing up and down the main street and being telephoned from house to house. One of the items was that the stage for Katma had failed to reach the roadhouse at Smith's Crossing. The message had come over the long-distance telephone early in the morning. The keeper of the roadhouse added his private fears that the stage, crawling up the divide as the blizzard swept down, must have gone astray and its occupants perished. The second bit of news was local. For the first time since Robert Milton had been cashier the bank had failed to open on the dot. The snow had not been cleared from the walk in front and no smoke was pouring from the chimney of the building.

CHAPTER XXIV
MACDONALD FOLLOWS A CLUE

Macdonald was no sluggard. It was his habit not to let the pleasure of the night before interfere with the business of the morning after. But in the darkness he overslept and let the town waken before him. He was roused by the sound of knocking on his door.

"Who is it?" he asked.

"It's me—Jones—Gopher Jones. Say, Mac, the bank ain't open and we can't rouse Milton. Thought I'd come to you, seeing as you're president of the shebang."

The mine-owner got up and began to dress. "Probably overslept, same as I did."

"That's the point. We looked through the window of his bedroom and his bed ain't been slept in."

In three minutes Macdonald joined the marshal and walked down with him to the bank. He unlocked the front door and turned to the little crowd that had gathered.

"Better wait here, boys. Gopher and I will go in. I expect everything is all right, but we'll let you know about that as soon as we find out."

The bank president opened the door, let the officer enter, and followed himself.

The sun had not yet risen and the blinds were down. Macdonald struck a match and held it up. The wood burned and the flame flickered out.

"Bank's been robbed," he announced quietly.

"Looks like," agreed Jones. His voice was uneven with excitement.

The Scotch-Canadian lit another match. In the flare of it they saw that the steel grill cutting off the alcove was open and that the door had been blown from the safe. It lay on the floor among a litter of papers, silver, fragments of steel, and bits of candle.

The marshal clutched at the arm of the banker. "Did you see—that?" he whispered.

His finger pointed through the darkness to the other end of the room. In the faint gray light of coming day Macdonald could see a huddled mass on the floor.

"There has been murder done. I'll get a light. Don't move from here, Jones. I want to look at things before we disturb them. There's no danger. The robbers have been gone for hours."

Gopher had as much nerve as the next man— when the sun was shining and he could see what danger he was facing. But there was something sinister and nerve-racking here. He wanted to throw open the door and shout the news to those outside.

By the light of another match the mine-owner crossed the room into the sitting-room of the cashier. Presently he returned with a lamp and let its light fall upon the figure lying slumped against the wall. A revolver lay close to the inert fingers. The head hung forward grotesquely upon the breast.

The dead man was Milton. His employer saw nothing ridiculous in the twisted neck and sprawling limbs. The cashier had died to save the money entrusted to his care.

Macdonald handed the lamp to the marshal and picked up the revolver. Every chamber was loaded.

"They beat him to it. They were probably here when he reached home. My guess is he heard them right away, got his gun, and came in. He's still wearing his dress suit. That gives us the time, for he left the club about midnight. Soon as they saw him they dropped him. Likely they heard him and were ready. I wouldn't have had this happen for all the money in the safe."

"How much was there in it?"

"I don't know exactly. The books will show. I'll send Wally down to look them over."

"Shot right spang through the heart, looks like," commented Jones, following with his eye the course of the wound.

"Wish I'd been here instead of him," Macdonald said grimly. His eyes softened as he continued to look down at the employee who had paid with his life for his faithfulness. "It wasn't an even break. Poor old fellow! You weren't built for a job like this, Robert Milton, but you played your hand out to a finish. That's all any man can do."

He turned abruptly away and began examining the safe. The silver still stood sacked in one large compartment. The bank-notes had escaped the hurried search of the robbers, but the gold was practically all gone. One sack had been torn by the explosion and single pieces of gold could be found all over the safe.

Macdonald glanced over the papers rapidly. The officer picked up one of dozens scattered over the floor. It was a mortgage note made out to the bank by a miner. He collected the others. Evidently the bandits had torn off the rubber, glanced over one or two to see if they had any cash value, and tossed the package into the air as a disgusted gambler does a pack of cards.

The bank president stepped to the door and threw it open. He explained the situation in three sentences.

"I can't let you in now, boys, until the coroner has been here," he went on to tell the crowd. "But there is one way you can all help. Keep your eyes open. If you have seen any suspicious characters around, let me know. Or if any one has left town in a hurry—or been seen doing anything during the night that you did not understand at the time. Men can't do a thing like this without leaving some clue behind them even though the snow has wiped away their trail."

A man named Fred Tague pushed to the front. He kept a feed corral near the edge of town. "I can tell you one man who mushed out before five o'clock this morning—and that's Gid Holt."

The eyes of Macdonald, cold and hard as jade, fastened to the man. "How do you know?"

"That dog team he bought from Tim Ryan— Well, he's been keeping it in my corral. When I got there this morning it was gone. The snow hadn't wiped out the tracks of the runners yet, so he couldn't have left more than fifteen minutes before."

"What time was it when you reached the corral?"

"Might have been six—maybe a little later."

"You don't know that Holt took the team himself?"

"Come to that, I don't. But he had a key to the barn where the sled was. Holt has been putting up at the hotel. I reckon it is easy to find out if he's still there."

Macdonald's keen brain followed the facts as the nose of a bloodhound does a trail. Holt, an open enemy of his, had reached town only two days before. He had bought one of the best and swiftest dog teams in the North and had let slip before witnesses the remark that Macdonald would soon find out what he wanted with the outfit. The bank had been robbed after midnight. To file open the grill and to blow up the safe must have taken several hours. Before morning the dogs of Holt had taken the trail. If their owner were with them, it was a safe bet that the sled carried forty thousand dollars in Alaska gold dust.

So far the mind of the Scotchman followed the probabilities logically, but at this point it made a jump. There were at least two robbers. He was morally sure of that, for this was not a one-man job. Now, if Holt had with him a companion, who of all those in Kusiak was the most likely man? He was a friendless, crabbed old fellow. Since coming to Kusiak old Gideon had been seen constantly with one man. Together they had driven out the day before and tried his new team. They had been with each other at dinner and had later left the hotel together. The name of the man who had been so friendly with old Holt was Gordon Elliot—and Elliot not only was another enemy of Macdonald, but had very good reasons for getting out of the country just now.

The strong jaw of the mine-owner stood out saliently as he gave short, sharp orders to men in the crowd. One was to get the coroner, a second Wally Selfridge, another the United States District Attorney. He divided the rest into squads to guard the roads leading out of town and to see that nobody passed for the present.

As soon as the men he had sent for arrived, Macdonald went over the scene of the crime with them. It was plain that the dynamiting had been done by an old-time miner who knew his business, but there had been brains in the planning of the robbery.

"There is no ivory above the ears of the man who bossed this job," Macdonald told the others. "He picks a night when we're all at the club, more than half a mile from here, a stormy night when folks are not wandering the streets. He knows that the wind will deaden the sound of the dynamite and that the snow will wipe out any tracks that might help to identify him and his pal or show which way they have gone."

The coroner took charge of the body and Wally of the bank. The mine-owner and the district attorney walked up to the hotel together. As soon as they had explained what they wanted, the landlord got a passkey and took them to the room Holt had used.

Apparently the bed had been slept in. In the waste-paper basket the district attorney found something which he held up in a significant silence. Macdonald stepped forward and took from him a small cloth sack.

"One of those we keep our gold in at the bank," said the Scotchman after a close examination.

"This definitely ties up Holt with the robbery. Now for Elliot."

"He left the hotel with Holt about five this morning the porter says." This was the contribution of the landlord.

The room of Gordon Elliot was in great disorder. Garments had been tossed on the bed and on every chair and had been left to lie wherever they had chanced to fall. Plainly their owner had been in great haste.

Macdonald looked through the closet where clothes hung. "His new fur coat is not here—nor his trail boots. Looks to me as though Mr. Gordon had hit the trail with his friend Holt."

This opinion was strengthened when it was learned from a store-owner in town that Holt and Elliot had routed him out of bed in the early morning to sell them two weeks' supplies. These they had packed upon the sled outside the store.

"It's a cinch bet that Elliot took the trail with him," the lawyer conceded.

All doubt of this was removed when a prospector reached town with the news that he had met Holt and Elliot traveling toward the divide as fast as they could drive the dogs.

The big Scotchman ordered his team of Siberian wolf-hounds made ready for the trail. As he donned his heavy furs, Colby Macdonald smiled with deep satisfaction. He had Elliot on the run at last.

Just as he closed the door of his room, Macdonald heard the telephone bell ring. He hesitated, then shrugged his shoulders and strode out into the storm. If he had answered the call he would have learned from Diane, who was at the other end of the line, that the stage upon which Sheba had started for Katma had not reached the roadhouse at Smith's Crossing.

Five minutes later the winners of the great Alaska Sweepstakes were flying down the street in the teeth of the storm. Armed with a rifle and a revolver, their owner was mushing into the hills to bring back the men who had robbed his bank and killed the cashier. He traveled alone because he could go faster without a companion. It never occurred to him that he was not a match for any two men he might face.

CHAPTER XXV
IN THE BLIZZARD

"Swiftwater" Pete, the driver of the stage between Kusiak and Katma, did not like the look of the sky as his ponies breasted the long uphill climb that ended at the pass. It was his habit to grumble. He had been complaining ever since they had started. But as he studied the heavy billows of cloud banked above the peaks and in the saddle between, there was real anxiety in his red, apoplectic face.

"Gittin' her back up for a blizzard, looks like. Doggone it, if that wouldn't jest be my luck," he murmured fretfully.

Sheba hoped there would be one, not, of course, a really, truly blizzard such as Macdonald had told her about, but the tail of a make-believe one, enough to send her glowing with exhilaration into the roadhouse with the happy sense of an adventure achieved. The girl had got out to relieve the horses, and as her young, lissom body took the hill scattering flakes of snow were already flying.

To-day she was buoyed up by a sense of freedom. For a time, at least, she was escaping Macdonald's driving energy, the appeal of

265

Gordon Elliot's warm friendliness, and the unvoiced urging of Diane. Good old Peter and the kiddies were the only ones that let her alone.

She looked back at the horses laboring up the hill. Swiftwater had got down and was urging them forward, his long whip crackling about the ears of the leaders. He waddled as he walked. His fat legs were too short for the round barrel body. A big roll of fat bulged out over the collar of his shirt. Whenever he was excited—and he always was on the least excuse—he puffed and snorted and grew alarmingly purple.

"Fat chance," he exploded as soon as he got within hearing. "Snow in those clouds—tons of it. H'm! And wind. Wow! We're in for an honest-to-God blizzard, sure as you're a foot high."

Swiftwater was worried. He would have liked to turn and run for it. But the last roadhouse was twenty-seven miles back. If the blizzard came howling down the slope they would have a sweet time of it reaching safety. Smith's Crossing was on the other side of the divide, only nine miles away. They would have to worry through somehow. Probably those angry clouds were half a bluff.

The temperature was dropping rapidly. Already snow fell fast in big thick flakes. To make it worse, the wind was beginning to rise. It came in shrill gusts momentarily increasing in force.

The stage-driver knew the signs of old and

cursed the luck that had led him to bring the stage. It was to have been the last trip with horses until spring. His dogs were waiting for him at Katma for the return journey. He did not blame himself, for there was no reason to expect such a storm so early in the season. None the less, it was too bad that his lead dog had been ailing when he left the gold camp eight days before.

Miss O'Neill knew that Swiftwater Pete was anxious, and though she was not yet afraid, the girl understood the reason for it. The road ran through the heart of a vast snow-field, the surface of which was being swept by a screaming wind. The air was full of sifted white dust, and the road furrow was rapidly filling. Soon it would be obliterated. Already the horses were panting and struggling as they ploughed forward. Sheba tramped behind the stage-driver and in her tracks walked Mrs. Olson, the other passenger.

Through the muffled scream of the storm Swiftwater shouted back to Sheba. "You wanta keep close to me."

She nodded her head. His order needed no explanation. The world was narrowing to a lane whose walls she could almost touch with her fingers. A pall of white wrapped them. Upon them beat a wind of stinging sleet. Nothing could be seen but the blurred outlines of the stage and the driver's figure.

The bitter cold searched through Sheba's furs

to her soft flesh and the blast of powdered ice beat upon her face. The snow was getting deeper as the road filled. Once or twice she stumbled and fell. Her strength ebbed, and the hinges of her knees gave unexpectedly beneath her. How long was it, she asked herself, that Macdonald had said men could live in a blizzard?

Staggering blindly forward, Sheba bumped into the driver. He had drawn up to give the horses a moment's rest before sending them plunging at the snow again.

"No chance," he called into the young woman's ear. "Never make Smith's in the world. Goin' try for miner's cabin up gulch little way."

The team stuck in the drifts, fought through, and was blocked again ten yards beyond. A dozen times the horses gave up, answered the sting of the whip by diving head first at the white banks, and were stopped by fresh snow-combs.

Pete gave up the fight. He began unhitching the horses, while Sheba and Mrs. Olson, clinging to each other's hands, stumbled forward to join him. The words he shouted across the back of a horse were almost lost in the roar of the shrieking wind.

". . . heluvatime . . . ride . . . gulch," Sheba made out.

He flung Mrs. Olson astride one of the wheelers and helped Sheba to the back of the right leader. Swiftwater clambered upon its mate himself.

The girl paid no attention to where they were going. The urge of life was so faint within her that she did not greatly care whether she lived or died. Her face was blue from the cold; her vitality was sapped. She seemed to herself to have turned to ice below the hips. Outside the misery of the moment her whole attention was concentrated on sticking to the back of the horse. Numb though her fingers were, she must keep them fastened tightly in the frozen mane of the animal. She recited her lesson to herself like a child. She must stick on—she must—she must.

Whether she lost consciousness or not Sheba never knew. The next she realized was that Swiftwater Pete was pulling her from the horse. He dragged her into a cabin where Mrs. Olson lay crouched on the floor.

"Got to stable the horses," he explained, and left them.

After a time he came back and lit a fire in the sheet-iron stove. As the circulation that meant life flooded back into her chilled veins Sheba endured a half-hour of excruciating pain. She had to clench her teeth to keep back the groans that came from her throat, to walk the floor and nurse her tortured hands with fingers in like plight.

The cabin was empty of furniture except for a home-made table, rough stools, and the frame of a bed. The last occupant had left a little firewood beside the stove, enough to last perhaps for twenty-four hours. Sheba did not need to be told that if the blizzard lasted long enough, they would starve to death. In the handbag left in the stage were a box of candy and an Irish plum pudding. She had brought the latter from the old country with her and was taking it and the chocolates to the Husted children. But just now the stage was as far from them as Drogheda.

Like many rough frontiersmen, Swiftwater Pete was a diamond in the raw. He had the kindly, gentle instincts that go to the making of a good man. So far as could be he made a hopeless and impossible situation comfortable. His judgment told him that they were caught in a trap from which there was no escape, but for the sake of the women he put a cheerful face on things.

"Lucky we found this cabin," he growled amiably. "By this time we'd 'a' been up Salt Creek if we hadn't. Seeing as our luck has stood up so far, I reckon we'll be all right. Mighty kind of Mr. Last Tenant to leave us this firewood. Comes to a showdown we've got one table, four stools, and a bed that will make first-class fuel. We ain't so worse off."

"If we only had some food," Mrs. Olson suggested.

"Food!" Pete looked at her in assumed surprise. "Huh! What about all that livestock I got in the stable? I've heard tell, ma'am, that broncho tenderloin is a favorite dish with them there

270

French chiefs that do the cooking. They kinder trim it up so's it's 'most as good as frawgs' legs."

Sheba had never before slept on bare boards with a sealskin coat for a sleeping-bag. But she was very tired and dropped off almost instantly. Twice she woke during the night, disturbed by the stiffness and the pain of her body. It seemed to her that the hard, whipsawed planks were pushing through the soft flesh to the bones. She was cold, too, and crept closer to the stout Swedish woman lying beside her. Presently she fell asleep again to the sound of the blizzard howling outside. When she wakened for the third time it was morning.

In the afternoon the blizzard died away. As far as she could see, Sheba looked out upon a waste of snow. Her eyes turned from the desolation without to the bare and cheerless room in which they had found shelter. In spite of herself a little shiver ran down the spine of the girl. Had she come into this Arctic solitude to find her tomb?

Resolutely she brushed the gloomy thought from her mind and began to chat with Mrs. Olson. In a corner of the cabin Sheba had found a torn and disreputable copy of "Vanity Fair." The covers and the first forty pages were gone. A splash of what appeared to be tobacco juice defiled the last sheet. But the fortunes of Becky and Amelia had served to make her forget during the morning that she was hungry and likely to be much hungrier before another day had passed.

As soon as the storm had moderated enough to let him go out with safety, Swiftwater Pete had taken one of the horses for an attempt at trail-breaking.

"Me, I'm after that plum pudding. I gotta get a feed of oats from the stage for my bronchs too. The scenery here is sure fine, but it ain't what you would call nourishing. Huh! Watch our smoke when me and old Baldface git to bucking them drifts."

He had been gone two hours and the early dusk was already descending over the white waste when Sheba ventured out to see what had become of the stage-driver. But the cold was so bitter that she soon gave up the attempt to fight her way through the drifts and turned back to the cabin.

Sometime later Swiftwater Pete came stumbling into their temporary home. He was fagged to exhaustion but triumphant. Upon the table he dropped from the crook of his numbed arm two packages.

"The makings for a Christmas dinner," he said with a grin.

After he had taken off his mukluks and his frozen socks they wrapped him in their furs while he toasted before the stove. Mrs. Olson thawed out the pudding and the chocolates in the oven and made a kind of mush out of some oats Pete had saved from the horse feed. They ate their one-sided meal in high spirits. The freeze had saved their lives. If it held clear till to-morrow they could reach Smith's Crossing on the crust of the snow.

Swiftwater broke up the chairs for fuel and demolished the legs of the table, after which he lay down before the stove and fell at once into a sodden sleep.

Presently Mrs. Olson lay down on the bed and began to snore regularly. Sheba could not sleep. The boards tired her bones and she was cold. Sometimes she slipped into cat naps that were full of bad dreams. She thought she was walking on the snow-comb of a precipice and that Colby Macdonald pushed her from her precarious footing and laughed at her as she slid swiftly toward the gulf below. When she wakened with a start it was to find that the fire had died down. She was shivering from lack of cover. Quietly the girl replenished the fire and lay down again.

When she wakened with a start it was morning. A faint light sifted through the single window of the shack. Sheba whispered to the older woman that she was going out for a little walk.

"Be careful, dearie," advised Mrs. Olson. "I wouldn't try to go too far."

Sheba smiled to herself at the warning. It was not likely that she would go far enough to get lost with all these millions of tons of snow piled up around her in every direction.

She had come out because she was restless and was tired of the dingy and uncomfortable room. Without any definite intentions, she naturally followed the trail that Swiftwater had broken the day before. No wind stirred and the sky was clear. But it was very cold. The sun would not be up for half an hour.

As she worked her way down the gulch Sheba wondered whether the news of their loss had reached Kusiak. Were search parties out already to rescue them? Colby Macdonald had gone out into the blizzard years ago to save her father. Perhaps he might have been out all night trying to save her father's daughter. Peter would go, of course,—and Gordon Elliot. The work in the mines would stop and men would volunteer by scores. That was one fine thing about the North. It responded to the unwritten law that a man must risk his own life to save others.

But if the wires had come down in the storm Kusiak would not know they had not got through to Smith's Crossing. Swiftwater Pete spoke cheerfully about mushing to the roadhouse. But Sheba knew the snow would not bear the horses. They would have to walk, and it was not at all certain that Mrs. Olson could do so long a walk with the thermometer at forty or fifty below zero.

From a little knoll Sheba looked down upon the top of the stage three hundred yards below her, and while she stood there the promise of the new day was blazoned on the sky. It came with amazing beauty of green and primrose and amethyst, while the stars flickered out and the heavens took on the blue of sunrise. In a crotch between two peaks a faint golden glow heralded the sun. A circle of lovely rose-pink flushed the horizon.

Sheba had this much of the poet in her, that every sunrise was still a miracle. She drew a deep, slow breath of adoration and turned away. As she did so her eyes dilated and her body grew rigid.

Across the snow waste a man was coming. He was moving toward the cabin and must cross the trench close to her. The heart of the girl stopped, then beat wildly to make up the lost stroke. He had come through the blizzard to save her.

At that very instant, as if the stage had been set for it, the wonderful Alaska sun pushed up into the crotch of the peaks and poured its radiance over the Arctic waste. The pink glow swept in a tide of delicate color over the snow and transmuted it to millions of sparkling diamonds. The Great Magician's wand had recreated the world instantaneously.

CHAPTER XXVI
HARD MUSHING

Elliot and Holt left Kusiak in a spume of whirling, blinding snow. They traveled light, not more than forty pounds to the dog, for they wanted to make speed. It was not cold for Alaska. They packed their fur coats on the sled and wore waterproof parkas. On their hands were mittens of moosehide with duffel lining, on their feet mukluks above "German" socks. Holt had been a sour-dough miner too long to let his partner perspire from overmuch clothing. He knew the danger of pneumonia from a sudden cooling of the heat of the body.

Old Gideon took seven of his dogs, driving them two abreast. Six were huskies, rangy, muscular animals with thick, dense coats. They were in the best of spirits and carried their tails erect like their Malemute leader. Butch, though a Malemute, had a strong strain of collie in him. It gave him a sense of responsibility. His business was to see that the team kept strung out on the trail, and Butch was a past-master in the matter of discipline. His weight was ninety-three fighting pounds, and he could thrash in short order any dog in the team.

The snow was wet and soft. It clung to every-thing it touched. The dogs carried pounds of it in the tufts of hair that rose from their backs. An icy pyramid had to be knocked from the sled every half-hour. The snowshoes were heavy with white slush. Densely laden spruce boughs brushed the faces of the men and showered them with unexpected little avalanches.

They took turns in going ahead of the team and breaking trail. It was heavy, muscle-grinding work. Before noon they were both utterly fatigued. They dragged forward through the slush, lifting their laden feet sluggishly. They must keep going, and they did, but it seemed to them that every step must be the last.

Shortly after noon the storm wore itself out. The temperature had been steadily falling and now it took a rapid drop. They were passing through timber, and on a little slope they built with a good deal of difficulty a fire. By careful nursing they soon had a great bonfire going, in front of which they put their wet socks, mukluks, scarfs, and parkas to dry. The toes of the dogs had become packed with little ice balls. Gordon and Holt had to go carefully over the feet of each animal to dig these out.

The old-timer thawed out a slab of dried salmon till the fat began to frizzle and fed each husky a pound of the fish and a lump of tallow. He and Gordon made a pot of tea and ate some meat sandwiches they had brought with them to save cooking until night.

When they took the trail again it was in moccasins instead of mukluks. The weather was growing steadily colder and with each degree of fall in the thermometer the trail became easier.

"Mushing at fifty below zero is all right when it is all right," explained Holt in the words of the old prospector. "But when it isn't right it's hell."

"It is not fifty below yet, is it?"

"Nope. But she's on the way. When your breath makes a kinder crackling noise she's fifty."

Travel was much easier now. There was a crust on the snow that held up the dogs and the sled so that trail-breaking was not necessary. The little party pounded steadily over the barren hills. There was no sign of life except what they brought with them out of the Arctic silence and carried with them into the greater silence beyond. A little cloud of steam enveloped them as they moved, the moisture from the breath of nine moving creatures in a waste of emptiness.

Each of the men wrapped a long scarf around his mouth and nose for protection, and as the part in front of his face became a sheet of ice shifted the muffler to another place.

Night fell in the middle of the afternoon, but they kept traveling. Not till they were well up toward the summit of the divide did they decide to camp. They drove into a little draw and unharnessed the weary dogs. It was bitterly cold, but they were forced to set up the tent and stove to keep from freezing. Their numbed fingers made a slow job of the camp preparations. At last the stove was going, the dogs fed, and they themselves thawed out. They fell asleep shortly to the sound of the mournful howling of the dogs outside.

Long before daybreak they were afoot again. Holt went out to chop some wood for the stove while Gordon made breakfast preparations. The little miner brought in an armful of wood and went out to get a second supply. A few moments later Elliot heard a cry.

He stepped out of the tent and ran to the spot where Holt was lying under a mass of ice and snow. The young man threw aside the broken blocks that had plunged down from a ledge above.

"Badly hurt, Gid?" he asked.

"I done bust my laig, son," the old man answered with a twisted grin.

"You mean that it is broken?"

"Tell you that in a minute."

He felt his leg carefully and with Elliot's help tried to get up. Groaning, he slid back to the snow.

"Yep. She's busted," he announced.

Gordon carried him to the tent and laid him down carefully. The old miner swore softly.

"Ain't this a hell of a note, boy? You'll have to get me to Smith's Crossing and leave me there."

It was the only thing to be done. Elliot broke camp and packed the sled. Upon the load he put his companion, well wrapped up in furs. He harnessed the dogs and drove back to the road.

Two miles farther up the road Gordon stopped his team sharply. He had turned a bend in the trail and had come upon an empty stage buried in the snow.

The fear that had been uppermost in Elliot's mind for twenty-four hours clutched at his throat. Was it tragedy upon which he had come after his long journey?

Holt guessed the truth. "They got stalled and cut loose the horses. Must have tried to ride the cayuses to shelter."

"To Smith's Crossing?" asked Gordon.

"Expect so." Then, with a whoop, the man on the sled contradicted himself. "No, by Moses, to Dick Fiddler's old cabin up the draw. That's where Swiftwater would aim for till the blizzard was over."

"Where is it?" demanded his friend.

"Swing over to the right and follow the little gulch. I'll wait till you come back."

Gordon dropped the gee-pole and started on the instant. Eagerness, anxiety, dread fought in his heart. He knew that any moment now he might stumble upon the evidence of the sad story which is repeated in Alaska many times every winter. It rang in him like a bell that where tough, hardy miners succumbed a frail girl would have small chance.

He cut across over the hill toward the draw, and at what he saw his pulse quickened. Smoke was pouring out of the chimney of a cabin and falling groundward, as it does in the Arctic during very cold weather. Had Sheba found safety there? Or was it the winter home of a prospector?

As he pushed forward the rising sun flooded the earth with pink and struck a million sparkles of color from the snow. The wonder of it drew the eyes of the young man for a moment toward the hills.

A tumult of joy flooded his veins. The girl who held in her soft hands the happiness of his life stood looking at him. It seemed to him that she was the core of all that lovely tide of radiance. He moved toward her and looked down into the trench where she waited. Swiftly he kicked off his snowshoes and leaped down beside her.

The gleam of tears was in her eyes as she held out both hands to him. During the long look they gave each other something wonderful to both of them was born into the world.

When he tried to speak his hoarse voice broke. "Sheba—little Sheba! Safe, after all. Thank God, you—you—" He swallowed the lump in his throat and tried again. "If you knew—God, how I have suffered! I was afraid—I dared not let myself think."

A live pulse beat in her white throat. The tears brimmed over. Then, somehow, she was in his arms weeping. Her eyes slowly turned to his, and he met the touch of her surrendered lips.

Nature had brought them together by one of her resistless and unpremeditated impulses.

CHAPTER XXVII
TWO ON THE TRAIL

A stress of emotion had swept her into his arms. Now she drew away from him shyly. The conventions in which she had been brought up asserted themselves. Sheba remembered that they had been carried by the high wave of their emotion past all the usual preliminaries. He had not even told her that he loved her. An absurd little fear obtruded itself into her happiness. Had she rushed into his arms like a lovesick girl, taking it for granted that he cared for her?

"You—came to look for us?" she asked, with the little shy stiffness of embarrassment.

"For you—yes."

He could not take his eyes from her. It seemed to him that a bird was singing in his heart the gladness he could not express. He had for many hours pushed from his mind pictures of her lying white and rigid on the snow. Instead she stood beside him, her delicate beauty vivid as the flush of a flame.

"Did they telephone that we were lost?"

"Yes. I was troubled when the storm grew. I could not sleep. So I called up the roadhouse by long distance. They had not heard from the stage.

Later I called again. When I could stand it no longer, I started."

"Not on foot?"

"No. With Holt's dog team. He is back there. His leg is broken. A snow-slide crushed him this morning where we camped."

"Bring him to the cabin. I will tell the others you are coming."

"Have you had any food?" he asked.

A tired smile lit up the shadows of weariness under her soft, dark eyes. "Boiled oats, plum pudding, and chocolates," she told him.

"We have plenty of food on the sled. I'll bring it at once."

She nodded, and turned to go to the cabin. He watched for a moment the lilt in her walk. An expression from his reading jumped to his mind. Melodious feet! Some poet had said that, hadn't he? Surely it must have been Sheba of whom he was thinking, this girl so virginal of body and of mind, free and light-footed as a caribou on the hills.

Gordon returned to the sled and drove the team up the draw to the cabin. The three who had been marooned came to meet their rescuer.

"You must 'a' come right through the storm lickitty split," Swiftwater said.

"You're right we did. This side pardner of mine was hell-bent on wrestling with a blizzard," Holt answered dryly.

"Sorry you broke your laig, Gid."

"Then there's two of us sorry, Swiftwater. It's one of the best laigs I've got."

Sheba turned to the old miner impulsively. "If you could be knowing what I am thinking of you, Mr. Holt,—how full our hearts are of the gratitude—" She stopped, tears in her voice.

"Sho! No need of that, Miss. He dragged me along." His thumb jerked toward the man who was driving. "I've seen better dog punchers than Elliot, but he's got the world beat at routin' old-timers out of bed and persuadin' them to kick in with him and buck a blizzard. Me, o' course, I'm an old fool for comin'—"

The dark eyes of the girl were like stars in a frosty night. "Then you're the kind of a fool I love, Mr. Holt. I think it was just fine of you, and I'll never forget it as long as I live."

Mrs. Olson had cooked too long in lumber and mining camps not to know something about bone-setting. Under her direction Gordon made splints and helped her bandage the broken leg. Meanwhile Swiftwater Pete fed his horses from the grain on the sled and Sheba cooked an appetizing breakfast. The aroma of coffee and the smell of frying bacon stimulated appetites that needed no tempting.

Holt, propped up by blankets, ate with the others. For a good many years he had taken his luck as it came with philosophic endurance. Now he wasted no time in mourning what could not be helped. He was lucky the ice slide had not hit him in the head. A broken leg would mend.

While they ate, the party went into committee of the whole to decide what was best to be done. Gordon noticed that in all the tentative suggestions made by Holt and Swiftwater the comfort of Sheba was the first thing in mind.

The girl, too, noticed it and smilingly protested, her soft hand lying for the moment on the gnarled one of the old miner.

"It doesn't matter about me. We have to think of what will be best for Mr. Holt, of how to get him to the proper care. My comfort can wait."

The plan at last decided upon was that Gordon should make a dash for Smith's Crossing on snowshoes, where he was to arrange for a relief party to come out for the injured man and Mrs. Olson. He was to return at once without waiting for the rescuers. Next morning he and Sheba would start with Holt's dog team for Kusiak.

Macdonald had taught Sheba how to use snowshoes and she had been an apt pupil. From her suitcase she got out her moccasins and put them on. She borrowed the snowshoes of Holt, wrapped herself in her parka, and announced that she was going with Elliot part of the way.

Gordon thought her movements a miracle of supple lightness. Her lines had the swelling roundness of vital youth, her eyes were alive with the eagerness that time dulls in most faces. They spoke little as they swept forward over the white snow-wastes. The spell of the great North was over her. Its mystery was stirring in her heart, just as it had been when her lips had turned to his at the sunrise. As for him, love ran through his veins like old wine. But he allowed his feelings no expression. For though she had come to him of her own accord for that one blessed minute at dawn, he could not be sure what had moved her so deeply. She was treading a world primeval, the wonder of it still in her soft eyes. Would she waken to love or to disillusion?

He took care to see that she did not tire. Presently he stopped and held out his hand to say good-bye.

"Will you come back this way?" she asked.

"Yes. I ought to get here soon after dark. Will you meet me?"

She gave him a quick, shy little nod, turned without shaking hands, and struck out for the cabin. All through the day happiness flooded her heart. While she waited on Holt or helped Mrs. Olson cook or watched Swiftwater while he put up the tent in the lee of the cabin, little snatches of song bubbled from her lips. Sometimes they were bits of old Irish ballads that popped into her mind. Once, while she was preparing some coffee for her patient, it was a stanza from Burns:—

"Till a' the seas gang dry, my dear,
    And the rocks melt wi' the sun:
I will luve thee still, my dear,
    While the sands o' life shall run."

She caught old Gideon looking at her with a queer little smile on his weather-tanned face and she felt the color beat into her cheeks.

"I haven't bought a wedding present for twenty years," he told her presently, apropos of nothing that had been said. "I won't know what's the proper thing to get, Miss Sheba."

"If you talk nonsense like that I'll go out and talk to Mr. Swiftwater Pete," she threatened, blushing.

Old Gid folded his hands meekly. "I'll be good—honest I will. Let's see. I got to make safe and sane conversation, have I? Hm! Wonder when that lazy, long-legged, good-for-nothing horsethief and holdup that calls himself Gordon Elliot will get back to camp."

Sheba looked into his twinkling eyes suspiciously as she handed him his coffee. For a moment she bit her lip to keep back a smile, then said with mock severity,—

"Now, I *am* going to leave you to Mrs. Olson."

When sunset came it found Sheba on the trail. Swiftwater Pete had offered to go with her, but she had been relieved of his well-meant kindness by the demand of Holt.

"No, you don't, Pete. You ain't a-goin' off gallivantin' with no young lady. You're a-goin' to stay here and fix my game laig for me. What do you reckon Miss Sheba wants with a fat, lopsided lummox like you along with her?"

Pete grew purple with embarrassment. He had not intended anything more than civility and he wanted this understood.

"Hmp! Ain't you got no sense a-tall, Gid? If Miss Sheba's hell-bent on goin' to meet Elliot, I allowed some one ought to go along and keep the dark offen her. 'Course there ain't nothin' going to harm her, unless she goes and gets lost—"

Sheba's smile cooled the heat of the stage-driver. "Which she isn't going to do. Good of you to offer to go with me. Don't mind Mr. Holt. Everybody knows he doesn't mean half of what he says. I'd be glad to have you come with me, but it isn't necessary at all. So I'll not trouble you."

Darkness fell quickly, but Sheba still held to the trail. There was no sign of Elliot, but she felt sure he would come soon. Meanwhile she followed steadily the tracks he had made earlier in the day.

She stopped at last. It was getting much colder. She was miles from the camp. Reluctantly she decided to return. Then, out of the darkness, he came abruptly upon her, the man whom she had come out to meet.

Under the magic of the Northern stars they

found themselves again in each other's arms for that brief moment of joyful surprise. Then, as it had been in the morning, Sheba drew herself shyly away.

"They are waiting supper for us," she told him irrelevantly.

He did not shout out his happiness and tell her to let them wait. For Gordon, too, felt awed at this wonderful adventure of love that had befallen them. It was enough for him that they were moving side by side, alone in the deep snows and the biting cold, that waves of emotion crashed through his pulses when his swinging hand touched hers.

They were acutely conscious of each other. Excitement burned in the eyes that turned to swift, reluctant meetings. She was a woman, and he was her lover. Neither of them dared quite accept the fact yet, but it filled the background of all their thoughts with delight.

Sheba did not want to talk of this new, amazing thing that had come into her life. It was too sacred a subject to discuss just yet even with him. So she began to tell him odd fancies from childhood that lingered in her Celtic heart, tales of the "little folk" that were half memories and half imaginings, stirred to life by some odd association of sky and stars. She laughed softly at herself as she told them, but Gordon did not laugh at her.

Everything she did was for him divinely done. Even when his eyes were on the dark trail ahead he saw only the dusky loveliness of curved cheek, the face luminous with a radiance some women are never privileged to know, the rhythm of head and body and slender legs that was part of her individual, heaven-sent charm.

The rest had finished supper before Gordon and Sheba reached camp, but Mrs. Olson had a hot meal waiting for them.

"I fixed up the tent for the women folks — stove, sleeping-bags, plenty of wood. Touch a match to the fire and it'll be snug as a bug in a rug," explained Swiftwater to Gordon.

Elliot and Sheba were to start early for Kusiak and later the rescue party would arrive to take care of Holt and Mrs. Olson.

"Time to turn in," Holt advised. "You better light that stove, Elliot."

The young man was still in the tent arranging the sleeping-bags when Sheba entered. He tried to walk out without touching her, intending to call back his good-night. But he could not do it. There was something flamey about her to-night that went to his head. Her tender, tremulous little smile and the turn of the buoyant little head stirred in him a lover's rhapsody.

"It's to be a long trail we cover to-morrow, Sheba. You must sleep. Good-night."

"Good-night—Gordon."

There was a little flash of audacity in the whimsical twist of her mouth. It was the first time she had ever called him by his given name.

Elliot threw away prudence and caught her by the hands.

"My dear—my dear!" he cried.

She trembled to his kiss, gave herself to his embrace with innocent passion. Tendrils of hair, fine as silk, brushed his cheeks and sent strange thrills through him.

They talked the incoherent language of lovers that is compounded of murmurs and silences and the touch of lips and the meetings of eyes. There were to be other nights in their lives as rich in memories as this, but never another with quite the same delight.

Presently Sheba reminded him with a smile of the long trail he had mentioned. Mrs. Olson bustled into the tent, and her presence stressed the point.

"Good-night, neighbors," Gordon called back from outside the tent.

Sheba's "Good-night" echoed softly back to him.

The girl fell asleep to the sound of the light breeze slapping the tent and to the doleful howling of the huskies.

CHAPTER XXVIII
A MESSAGE FROM THE DEAD

Macdonald drove his team into the teeth of the storm. The wind came in gusts. Sometimes the gale was so stiff that the dogs could scarcely crawl forward against it; again there were moments of comparative stillness, followed by squalls that slapped the driver in the face like the whipping of a loose sail on a catboat.

High drifts made the trail difficult. Not once but fifty times Macdonald left the gee-pole to break a way through snow-waves for the sled. The best he could get out of his dogs was three miles an hour, and he knew that there was not another team or driver in the North could have done so well.

It was close to noon when he reached a division of the road known as the Fork. One trail ran down to the river and up it to the distant creeks. The other led across the divide, struck the Yukon, and pointed a way to the coast. White drifts had long since blotted out the track of the sled that had preceded him. Had the fugitives gone up the river to the creeks with intent to hole themselves up for the winter? Or was it their purpose to cross the divide and go out over the ice to the coast?

The pursuer knew that Gid Holt was wise as a weasel. He could follow blindfolded the paths that led to every creek in the gold-fields. It might be taken as a certainty that he had not plunged into such a desperate venture without having a plan well worked out beforehand. Elliot had a high grade of intelligence. Would they try to reach the coast and make their getaway to Seattle? Or would they dig themselves in till the heavy snows were past and come back to civilization with the story of a lucky strike to account for the gold they brought with them? Neither gold-dust nor nuggets could be identified. There would be no way of proving the story false. The only evidence against them would be that they had left at Kusiak and this was merely of a corroborative kind. There would be no chance of convicting them upon it.

But to strike for Seattle was to throw away all pretense of innocence. Fugitives from justice, they would have to disappear from sight in order to escape. The hunt for them would continue until at last they were unearthed.

One fork of the road led to comparative safety; the other went by devious windings to the penitentiary and perhaps the gallows. The Scotchman put himself in the place of the men he was trailing. Given the same conditions, he knew which path he would follow.

Macdonald took the trail that led down to the

river, to the distant gold-creeks which offered a refuge from man-hunters in many a deserted cabin marooned by the deep snows.

Even the iron frame and steel muscles of the Scotch-Canadian protested against the task he had set them that day. It was a time to sit snugly inside by a stove and listen to the howling of the wind as it hurled itself down from the divide. But from daylight till dark Colby Macdonald fought with drifts and breasted the storm. He got into the harness with the dogs. He broke trail for them, cheered them, soothed, comforted, punished. Long after night had fallen he staggered into the hut of two prospectors, his parka so stiff with frozen snow that it had to be beaten with a hammer before the coat could be removed.

"How long since a dog team passed—seven huskies and two men?" was his first question.

"No dog team has passed for four days," one of the men answered.

"You mean you haven't seen one," Macdonald corrected.

"I mean none has passed—unless it went by in the night while we slept. And even then our dogs would have warned us."

Macdonald flung his ice-coated gloves to a table and stooped to take off his mukluks. His face was blue with the cold, but the bleak look in the eyes came from within. He said nothing more until he was free of his wet clothes. Then he sat down heavily and passed a hand over his frozen eyebrows.

"Get me something to eat and take care of my dogs. There is food for them on the sled," he said.

While he ate he told them of the bank robbery and the murder. Their resentment against the men who had done it was quite genuine. There could be no doubt they told the truth when they said no sled had preceded his. They were honest, reliable prospectors. He knew them both well.

The weary man slept like a log. He opened his eyes next morning to find one of his hosts shaking him.

"Six o'clock, Mr. Macdonald. Your breakfast is ready. Jim is looking out for the huskies."

Half an hour later the Scotchman gave the order, "Mush!" He was off again, this time on the back trail as far as the Narrows, from which point he meant to strike across to intersect the fork of the road leading to the divide.

The storm had passed and when the late sun rose it was in a blue sky. Fine enough the day was overhead, but the slushy snow, where it was worn thin on the river by the sweep of the wind, made heavy travel for the dogs. Macdonald was glad enough to reach the Narrows, where he could turn from the river and cut across to hit the trail of the men he was following. He had about five miles to go before he would reach the Smith Crossing road and every foot of it he would have to break trail for the dogs. This was slow business, since he had no partner at the gee-pole. Back and forth, back and forth he trudged, beating down the loose snow for the runners. It was a hill trail, and the drifts were in most places not very deep. But the Scotchman was doing the work of two, and at a killing pace.

Over a ridge the team plunged down into a little park where the snow was deeper. Macdonald, breaking trail across the mountain valley, found his feet weighted with packed ice slush so that he could hardly move them. When at last he had beaten down a path for his dogs he stood breathing deep at the summit of the slope. Before him lay the main road to Smith's Crossing, scarce fifty yards away. He gave a deep whoop of triumph, for along it ran the wavering tracks left by a sled. He was on the heels of his enemy at last.

As he turned back to his Siberian hounds, the eyes of Macdonald came to abrupt attention. On the hillside, not ten yards from him, something stuck out of the snow like a signpost. It was the foot of a man.

Slowly Macdonald moved toward it. He knew well enough what he had stumbled across—one of the tragedies that in the North are likely to be found in the wake of every widespread blizzard. Some unfortunate traveler, blinded by the white swirl, had wandered from the trail and had staggered up a draw to his death.

With a little digging the Alaskan uncovered a leg. The man had died where he had fallen, face down. Macdonald scooped away the snow and found a pack strapped to the back of the buried man. He cut the thongs and tried to ease it away. But the gunnysack had frozen to the parka. When he pulled, the rotten sacking gave way under the strain. The contents of the pack spilled out.

The eyes in the grim face of Macdonald grew hard and steely. He had found, by some strange freak of chance, much more than he had expected to find. Using his snowshoe as a shovel, he dug the body free and turned it over. At sight of the face he gave a cry of astonishment.

CHAPTER XXIX

"DON'T TOUCH HIM! DON'T YOU DARE TOUCH HIM!"

Gordon overslept. His plan had been to reach Kusiak at the end of a long day's travel, but that had meant getting on the trail with the first gleam of light. When he opened his eyes Mrs. Olson was calling him to rise.

He dressed and stepped out into the cold, crisp morning. From the hill crotch the sun was already pouring down a great, fanlike shaft of light across the snow vista. Swiftwater Pete passed behind him on his way to the stable and called a cheerful good-morning in his direction.

Mrs. Olson had put the stove outside the tent and Gordon lifted it to the spot where they did the cooking.

"Good-morning, neighbor," he called to Sheba. "Sleep well?"

The little rustling sounds within the tent ceased. A face appeared in the doorway, the flaps drawn discreetly close beneath the chin.

"Never better. Is my breakfast ready yet?"

"Come and help me make it. Mrs. Olson is waiting on Holt."

"When I'm dressed." The smiling face disappeared. "Dublin Bay" sounded in her fresh young voice from the tent. Gordon joined in the song as he lit the fire and sliced bacon from a frozen slab of it.

The howling of the huskies interrupted the song. They had evidently heard something that excited them. Gordon listened. Was it in his fancy only that the breeze carried to him the faint jingle of sleigh-bells? The sound, if it was one, died away. The cook turned to his job.

He stopped sawing at the meat, knife and bacon both suspended in the air. On the hard snow there had come to him the crunch of a foot behind him. Whose? Sheba was in the tent, Swiftwater at the stable, Mrs. Olson in the house. Slowly he turned his head.

What Elliot saw sent the starch through his body. He did not move an inch, still sat crouched by the fire, but every nerve was at tension, every muscle taut. For he was looking at a rifle lying negligently in brown, steady hands. They were very sure hands, very competent ones. He knew that because he had seen them in action. The owner of the hands was Colby Macdonald.

The Scotch-Canadian stood at the edge of a willow grove. His face was grim as the day of judgment.

"Don't move," he ordered.

Elliot laughed irritably. He was both annoyed and disgusted.

"What do you want?" he snapped.

"You."

"What's worrying you now? Do you think I'm jumping my bond?"

"You're going back to Kusiak with me—to give a life for the one you took."

"What's that?" cried Gordon, surprised.

"Just as I'm telling you. I've been on your heels ever since you left town. You and Holt are going back with me as my prisoners."

"But what for?"

"For robbing the bank and murdering Robert Milton, as you know well enough."

"Is this another plant arranged for me by you and Selfridge?" demanded Elliot.

Macdonald ignored the question and lifted his voice. "Come out of that tent, Holt,—and come with your hands up unless you want your head blown off."

"Holt isn't in that tent, you damned idiot. If you want to know—"

"Come *now,* if you expect to come alive," cut in the Scotchman ominously. He raised the rifle to his shoulder and covered the shadow thrown by the sun on the figure within.

Gordon flung out a wild protest and threw the frozen slab of bacon at the head of Macdonald. With the same motion he launched his own body across the stove. A fifth of a second earlier the tent flap had opened and Sheba had come out.

The sight of her paralyzed Macdonald and saved her lover's life. It distracted the mine-owner long enough for him to miss his chance. A bullet struck the stove and went off at a tangent through the tent canvas not two feet from where Sheba stood. A second went speeding toward the sun. For Gordon had followed the football player's instinct and dived for the knees of his enemy.

They went down together. Each squirming for the upper place, they rolled over and over. The rifle was forgotten. Like cave men they fought, crushing and twisting each other's muscles with the blind lust of primordials to kill. As they clinched with one arm, they struck savagely with the other. The impact of smashing blows on naked flesh sounded horribly cruel to Sheba.

She ran forward, calling on each by name to stop. Probably neither knew she was there. Their whole attention was focused on each other. Not for an instant did their eyes wander, for life and death hung on the issue. Chance had lit the spark of their resentment, but long-banked passions were blazing fiercely now.

They got to their feet and fought toe to toe. Sledge-hammer blows beat upon bleeding and disfigured faces. No thought of defense as yet was in the mind of either. The purpose of each was to bruise, maim, make helpless the other. But for the impotent little cries of Sheba no sound broke the stillness save the crunch of their feet on the hard snow, the thud of heavy fists on flesh, and the throaty snarl of their deep, irregular breathing.

Gid Holt, from the window of the cabin, watched the battle with shining eyes. He exulted in every blow of Gordon; he suffered with him when the smashing rights and lefts of Macdonald got home. He shouted jeers, advice, threats, encouragement. If he had had ten thousand dollars wagered on the outcome he could not have been more excited.

Swiftwater Pete, drawn by the cries of Sheba, came running from the stable. As he passed the window, Holt caught him by the arm.

"What are you aimin' to do, Pete? Let 'em alone. Let 'em go to it. They got to have it out. Stop 'em now and they'll get at it with guns."

Sheba ran up, wringing her hands. "Stop them, please. They're killing each other."

"Nothing of the kind, girl. You let 'em alone, Pete. The kid's there every minute, ain't he? Gee, that's a good one, boy. Seven—eleven—ninety-two. 'Attaboy!"

Macdonald had slipped on the snow and gone down to his hands and knees. Swift as a wildcat the younger man was on top of him. Hampered though he was by his parka, the Scotchman struggled slowly to his feet again. He was much the heavier man, and in spite of his years the stronger. The muscles stood out in knots on his shoulders and across his back, whereas on the body of his more slender opponent they flowed and rippled in rounded symmetry. Active as a heather cat, Elliot was far the quicker of the two.

Half-blinded by the hammering he had received, Gordon changed his method of fighting. He broke away from the clinch and sidestepped the bull-like rush of his foe, covering up as well as he could from the onset. Macdonald pressed the attack and was beaten back by hard, straight lefts and rights to the unprotected face.

The mine-owner shook the matted hair from his swollen eyes and rushed again. He caught an uppercut flush on the end of the chin. It did not even stop him. The weight of his body was in the blow he lashed up from his side.

The knees of Elliot doubled up under him like the blade of a jackknife. He sank down slowly, turned, got to his hands and knees, and tried to shake off the tons of weight that seemed to be holding him down.

Macdonald seized him about the waist and flung him to the ground. Upon the inert body the victor dropped, his knees clinching the torso of the unconscious man.

"Now, Pete. Go to him," urged Holt wildly.

But before Swiftwater could move, before the great fist of Macdonald could smash down upon the bleeding face upturned to his, a sharp blow struck the flesh of the raised forearm and for the moment stunned the muscles. The Scotch-Canadian lifted a countenance drunk with rage, passion-tossed.

Slowly the light of reason came back into his eyes. Sheba was standing before him, his rifle in her hand. She had struck him with the butt of it.

"Don't touch him! Don't you dare touch him!" she challenged.

He looked at her long, then let his eyes fall to the battered face of his enemy. Drunkenly he got to his feet and leaned against a willow. His forces were spent, his muscles weighted as with lead. But it was not this alone that made his breath come short and raggedly.

Sheba had flung herself down beside her lover. She had caught him tightly in her arms so that his disfigured face lay against her warm bosom. In the eyes lifted to those of the mine-owner was an unconquerable defiance.

"He's mine—mine, you murderer," she panted fiercely. "If you kill him, you must kill me first."

The man she had once promised to marry was looking at a different woman from the girl he had known. The soft, shy youth of her was gone. She was a forest mother of the wilds ready to fight for her young, a wife ready to go to the stake for the husband of her choice. An emotion primitive and poignant had transformed her.

His eyes burned at her the question his parched lips and throat could scarcely utter. "So you . . . love him?"

But though it was in form a question he knew already the answer. For the first time in his life he began to taste the bitterness of defeat. Always he had won what he coveted by brutal force or his stark will. But it was beyond him to compel the love of a girl who had given her heart to another.

"Yes," she answered.

Her hair in two thick braids was flung across her shoulders, her dark head thrown back proudly from the rounded throat.

Macdonald smiled, but there was no mirth in his savage eyes. "Do you know what I want with him—why I have come to get him?"

"No."

"I've come to take him back to Kusiak to be hanged because he murdered Milton, the bank cashier."

The eyes of the woman blazed at him. "Are you mad?"

"It's the truth." Macdonald's voice was curt and harsh. "He and Holt were robbing the bank when Milton came back from the dance at the club. The cowards shot down the old man like a dog. They'll hang for it if it costs me my last penny, so help me God."

"You say it's the truth," she retorted scornfully. "Do you think I don't know you now—how you twist and distort facts to suit your ends? How long is it since your jackal had him arrested for assaulting you—when Wally Selfridge knew—and you knew—that he had risked his life for you and had saved yours by bringing you to Diane's after he had bandaged your wounds?"

"That was different. It was part of the game of politics we were playing."

"You admit that you and your friends lied then. Is it like you could persuade me that you're telling the truth now?"

The big Alaskan shrugged. "Believe it or not as you like. Anyhow, he's going back with me to Kusiak—and Holt, too, if he's here."

An excited cackle cut into the conversation, followed by a drawling announcement from the window. "Your old tillicum is right here, Mac. What's the use of waiting? Why don't you have your hanging-bee now?"

CHAPTER XXX
HOLT FREES HIS MIND

Macdonald whirled in his tracks.

Old Gid Holt was leaning on his elbow with his head out of the window. "You better come and beat me up first, Mac," he jeered. "I'm all stove up with a busted laig, so you can wollop me good. I'd come out there, but I'm too crippled to move."

"You're not too crippled to go back to Kusiak with me. If you can't walk, you'll ride. But back you go."

"Fine. I been worrying about how to get there. It's right good of you to bring one of these here taxis for me, as the old sayin' is."

"Where is the rest of the gold you stole?"

"I ain't seen the latest papers, Mac. What is this stuff about robbin' a bank and shootin' Milton?"

"You're under arrest for robbery and murder."

"Am I? Unload the particulars. When did I do it all?"

"You know when. Just before you left town."

Holt shook his head slowly. "No, sir. I can't seem to remember it. Sure it ain't some one else you're thinking about? Howcome you to fix on me as one of the bold, bad bandits?"

"Because you had not sense enough to cover your tracks. You might just as well have left a note saying you did it. First, you come to town and buy one of the fastest dog teams in Alaska. Why?"

"That's an easy one. I bought that team to win the Alaska Sweepstakes from you. And I'm goin' to do it. The team wasn't handled right or it would have won last time. I got to millin' it over and figured that old Gid Holt was the dog puncher that could land those huskies in front. See?"

"You bought it to make your getaway after the robbery," retorted Macdonald.

"It's a difference of opinion makes horse races. What else have you got against us?"

"We found in your room one of the sacks that had held the gold you took from the bank."

"That's right. I took it from the bank in the afternoon, where I had had it on deposit, to pay for the team I bought. Milton's books will show that. But you didn't find any sack I took when your bank was robbed—if it was robbed," added the old man significantly.

"Of course, I knew you would have an alibi. Have you got one to explain why you left town so suddenly the night the bank was robbed? Milton was killed after midnight. Before morning you and your friend Elliot routed out Ackroyd and bought a lot of supplies from him for a hurry-up

312

trip. You slipped around to the corral and hit the trail right into the blizzard. Will you tell me why you were in such a hurry to get away, if it wasn't to escape from the town where you had murdered a decent old fellow who never had harmed a soul?"

"Sure I'll tell you." The black eyes of the little man snapped eagerly. "I came so p. d. q. because that side pardner of mine Gordon Elliot wouldn't let me wait till mornin'. He had a reason for leavin' town that wouldn't wait a minute, one big enough to drive him right into the heart of the blizzard. Me, I tagged along."

"I can guess his reason," jeered the Scotchman. "But I'd like to hear you put a name to it."

Holt grinned maliciously and waved a hand toward the girl who was pillowing the head of her lover. "The name of his reason is Sheba O'Neill, but it's goin' to be Sheba Elliot soon, looks like."

"You mean—"

The little miner took the words triumphantly out of his mouth. He leaned forward and threw them into the face of the man he hated. "I mean that while you was dancin' and philanderin' with other women, Gordon Elliot was buckin' a blizzard to save the life of the girl you both claimed to love. He was mushin' into fifty miles of frozen hell while you was fillin' up with potted grouse and champagne. Simultaneous with the lame goose and the monkey singlestep

313

you was doin,' this lad was windjammin' through white drifts. He beat you at your own game, man. You're a bear for the outdoor stuff, they tell me. You chew up a blizzard for breakfast and throttle a pack of wolves to work up an appetite for dinner. It's your specialty. All right. Take your hat off to that chechacko who has just whaled you blind. He has outgamed you, Colby Macdonald. You don't run in his class. I see he is holding his haid up again. Give him another half-hour and he'd be ready to go to the mat with you again."

The big Alaskan pushed away a fear that had been lingering in his mind ever since he had stumbled on that body buried in the snow yesterday afternoon. Was his enemy going to escape him, after all? Could Holt be telling the true reason why they had left town so hurriedly? He would not let himself believe it.

"You ought to work up a better story than that," he said contemptuously. "You can throw a husky through the holes in it. How could Elliot know, for instance, that Miss O'Neill was not safe?"

"The same way you could' a' known it," snapped old Gideon. "He 'phoned to Smith's Crossin' and found the stage hadn't got in and that there was a hell of a storm up in the hills."

Macdonald set his face. "You're lying to me. You stumbled over the stage while you were making your getaway. Now you're playing it for an alibi."

Elliot had risen. Sheba stood beside him, her hand in his. She spoke quietly.

"It's the truth. Believe it or not as you please. We care nothing about that."

The stab of her eyes, the carriage of the slim, pliant figure with its suggestion of fine gallantry, challenged her former lover to do his worst.

On the battered face of Gordon was a smile. So long as his Irish sweetheart stood by him he did not care if he were charged with high treason. It was worth all it cost to feel the warmth of her brave, impulsive trust.

The deep-set eyes of Macdonald clinched with those of his rival. "You cached the rest of the gold, I suppose," he said doggedly.

With a lift of his shoulders the younger man answered lightly. "There are none so blind as those who will not see, Mr. Macdonald." He turned to Sheba. "Come. We must make breakfast."

"You're going to Kusiak with me," his enemy said bluntly.

"After we have eaten, Mr. Macdonald," returned Elliot with an ironic bow. "Perhaps, if you have not had breakfast yet, you will join us."

"We start in half an hour," announced the mine-owner curtly, and he turned on his heel.

The rifle lay where Sheba had dropped it when she ran to gather her stricken lover into her arms. Macdonald picked it up and strode over the brow of the hill without a backward look. He was too proud to stay and watch them. It was impossible to escape him in the deep snow that filled the hill trails, and he was convinced they would attempt nothing of the kind.

The Scotchman felt for the first time in his life old and spent. Under tremendous difficulty he had mushed for two days and had at last run his men down. The lust of vengeance had sat on his shoulders every mile of the way and had driven him feverishly forward. But the salt that had lent a savor to his passion was gone. Even though he won, he lost. For Sheba had gone over to the enemy.

With the fierce willfulness of his temperament he tried to tread under foot his doubts about the guilt of Holt and Elliot. Success had made him arrogant and he was not a good loser. He hated the man who had robbed him of Sheba, but he could not escape respecting him. Elliot had fought until he had been hammered down into unconsciousness and he had crawled to his feet and stood erect with the smile of the unconquered on his lips. Was this the sort of man to murder in cold blood a kindly old gentleman who had never harmed him?

The only answer Macdonald found was that Milton had taken him and his partners by surprise. They had been driven to shoot the cashier to cover up their crime. Perhaps Holt or another had fired the actual shots, but Elliot was none the less guilty. The heart of the Scotchman was bitter within him. He intended to see that his enemies paid to the last ounce. He would harry them to the gallows if money and influence could do it.

None the less, his doubts persisted. If they had planned the bank robbery, why did they wait so long to buy supplies for their escape? Why had they not taken the river instead of the hill trail? The story that his enemies told hung together. It had the ring of truth. The facts supported it.

One piece of evidence in their favor Macdonald alone knew. It lay buried in the deep snows of the hills. He shut his strong teeth in the firm resolve that it should stay there.

CHAPTER XXXI
SHEBA DIGS

The weather had moderated a good deal, but the trail was a protected forest one. The two teams now going down had come up, so that the path was packed fairly hard and smooth. Holt lay propped on his own sled against the sleeping-bags. Sheba mushed behind Gordon. She chatted with them both, but ignored entirely the existence of Macdonald, who followed with his prize-winning Siberian dogs.

Though she tried not to let her lover know it, Sheba was troubled at heart. Gordon was practically the prisoner of a man who hated him bitterly, who believed him guilty of murder, and who would go through fire to bring punishment home to him. She knew the power of Macdonald. With the money back of him, he had for two years fought against and almost prevailed over a strong public opinion in the United States. He was as masterful in his hatred as in his love. The dominant, fighting figure in the Northwest, he trod his sturdy way through opposition like a Colossus.

Nor did she any longer have any illusions about him. He could be both ruthless and unscrupulous when it suited his purpose. As the day wore toward noon, her spirits drooped. She was tired physically, and this reacted upon her courage.

The warmer weather was spoiling the trail. It became so soft and mushy that though snowshoes were needed, they could not be worn on account of the heavy snow which clung to them every time a foot was lifted. They wore mukluks, but Sheba was wet to the knees. The spring had gone from her step. Her shoulders began to sag.

For some time Gordon's eye had been seeking a good place for a day camp. He found it in a bit of open timber above the trail, and without a word he swung his team from the path.

"Where are you going?" demanded Macdonald.

"Going to rest for an hour," was Elliot's curt answer.

Macdonald's jaw clamped. He strode forward through the snow beside the trail. "We'll see about that."

The younger man faced him angrily. "Can't you see she is done, man? There is not another mile of travel in her until she has rested."

The hard, gray eyes of the Alaskan took in the slender, weary figure leaning against the sled. On a soft and mushy trail like this, where every footstep punched a hole in the loose snow, the dogs could not travel with any extra weight. A few miles farther down they would come to a main-traveled road and the going would be better.

But till then she must walk. Macdonald gave way with a gesture of his hand and turned on his heel.

At the camp-fire Sheba dried her mukluks, stockings, caribou mitts, and short skirts. Too tired to eat, she forced herself to swallow a few bites and drank eagerly some tea. Gordon had brought blankets from the sled and he persuaded her to lie down for a few minutes.

"You'll call me soon if I should sleep," she said drowsily, and her eyes were closed almost before the words were off her lips.

When Macdonald came to order the start half an hour later, she was still asleep. "Give her another thirty minutes," he said gruffly.

Youth is resilient. Sheba awoke rested and ready for work.

While Gordon was untangling the dogs she was left alone for a minute with the mine-owner.

The hungry look in his eyes touched her. Impulsively she held out her hand.

"You're going to be fair, aren't you, Mr. Macdonald? Because you—don't like him—you won't—?"

He looked straight into the dark, appealing eyes. "I'm going to be fair to Robert Milton," he told her harshly. "I'm going to see his murderers hanged if it costs me every dollar I have in the world."

"None of us object to justice," she told him

321

proudly. "Gordon has nothing to fear if only the truth is told."

"Then why come to me?" he demanded.

She hesitated; then with a wistful little smile, spoke what was in her heart. "I'm afraid you won't do justice to yourself. You're good—and brave—and strong. But you're very willful and set. I don't want to lose my friend. I want to know that he is all I have believed him—a great man who stands for the things that are fine and clean and just."

"Then it is for my sake and not for his that you want me to drop the case against Elliot?" he asked ironically.

"For yours and for his, too. You can't hurt him. Nobody can really be hurt from outside— not unless he is a traitor to himself. And Gordon Elliot isn't that. He couldn't do such a thing as this with which you charge him. It is not in his nature. He can explain everything."

"I don't doubt that. He and his friend Holt are great little explainers."

In spite of his bitterness Sheba felt a change in him. She seemed to have a glimpse of his turbid soul engaged in battle. He turned away without shaking hands, but it struck her that he was not implacable.

While they were at luncheon half a dozen pack-mules laden with supplies for a telephone construction line outfit had passed. Their small, sharp-shod hoofs had punched sink-holes in the trail at every step. Instead of a smooth bottom the dogs found a slushy bog cut to pieces.

At the end of an hour of wallowing Macdonald called a halt.

"There is a cutoff just below here. It will save us nearly two miles, but we'll have to break trail. Swing to the right just below the big willow," he told Elliot. "I'll join you presently and relieve you on the job. But first Miss O'Neill and I are going for a little side trip."

All three of them looked at him in sharp surprise. Gordon opened his lips to answer and closed them again without speaking. Sheba had flashed a warning to him.

"I hope this trip isn't very far off the trail," she said quietly. "I'm just a wee bit tired."

"It's not far," the mine-owner said curtly.

He was busy unpacking his sled. Presently he found the dog moccasins for which he had been looking, repacked his sled, and fitted the shoes to the bleeding feet of the team leader. Elliot, suspicious and uncertain what to do, watched him at work, but at a signal from Sheba turned reluctantly away and drove down to the cutoff.

Macdonald turned his dogs out of the trail and followed a little ridge for perhaps a quarter of a mile. Sheba trudged behind him. She was full of wonder at what he meant to do, but she asked no questions. Some wise instinct was telling her to do exactly as he said.

From the sled he took a shovel and gave it to the young woman. "Dig just this side of the big rock—close to the root of the tree," he told her.

Sheba dug, and at the second stroke of the spade struck something hard. He stooped and pulled out a sack.

"Open it," he said. "Rip it with this knife."

She ran the knife along the coarse weave of the cloth. Fifteen or twenty smaller sacks lay exposed. Sheba looked up at Macdonald, a startled question in her eyes.

He nodded. "You've guessed it. This is part of the gold for which Robert Milton was murdered."

"But—how did it get here?"

"I buried it there yesterday. Come."

He led her around the rock. Back of it lay something over which was spread a long bit of canvas. The heart of Sheba was beating wildly.

The Scotchman looked at her from a rock-bound face. "Underneath this canvas is the body of one of the men who murdered Milton. He died more miserably than the man he shot. Half the gold stolen from the bank is in that gunnysack you have just dug up. If you'll tell me who has the other half, I'll tell you who helped him rob the bank."

"This man—who is he?" asked Sheba, almost

in a whisper. She was trembling with excitement and nervousness.

Macdonald drew back the cloth and showed the rough, hard face of a workingman.

"His name was Trelawney. I kicked him out of our camps because he was a troublemaker."

"He was one of the men that robbed you later!" she exclaimed.

"Yes. And now he has tried to rob me again and has paid for it with his life."

Her mind flashed back over the past. "Then his partner in this last crime must have been the same man—what's his name?—that was with him last time."

"Northrup." He nodded slowly. "I hate to believe it, but it is probably true. And he, too, is lying somewhere in this park covered with snow—if our guess is right."

"And Gordon—you admit he didn't do it?"

Again he nodded, sulkily. "No. He didn't do it."

Joy lilted in her voice. "So you've brought me here to tell me. Oh, I am glad, my friend, that you were so good. And it is like you to do it. You have always been the good friend to me."

The Scotchman smiled, a little wistfully. "You take a mean advantage of a man. You nurse him when he is ill—and are kind to him when he is well—and try to love him, though he is twice your age and more. Then, when his enemy is in his power, he finds he can't strike him down without striking you too. Take your young man, Sheba O'Neill, and marry him, and for God's sake, get him out of Alaska before I come to grips with him again. I'm not a patient man, and he's tried me sair. They say I'm a good hater, and I always thought it true. But what's the use of hating a man when your soft arms are round him for an armor?"

The fine eyes of the girl were wells of warm light. Her gladness was not for herself and her lover only, but for the friend that had been so nearly lost and was now found. He believed he had done it for her, but Sheba was sure his reasons lay deeper. He was too much of a man to hide evidence and let his rival be falsely accused of murder. It was not in him to do a cheap thing like that. When it came to the pinch, he was too decent to stab in the back. But she was willing to take him on his own ground.

"I'll always be thanking you for your goodness to me," she told him simply.

He brushed that aside at once. "There's one thing more, lass. I'll likely not be seeing you again alone, so I'll say it now. Don't waste any tears on Colby Macdonald. Don't fancy any story-book foolishness about spoiling his life. That may be true of halfling boys, maybe, but a man goes his ain gait even when he gets a bit facer."

"Yes," she agreed. And in a flash she saw what would happen, that in the reaction from his depression he would turn to Genevieve Mallory and marry her.

"You're too young for me, anyhow,—too soft and innocent. Once you told me that you couldn't keep step with me. It's true. You can't. It was a daft dream."

He took a deep breath, seemed to shake himself out of it, and smiled cheerfully upon her.

"We'll put our treasure-trove on the sled and go back to your friends," he continued briskly. "To-morrow I'll send men up to scour the hills for Northrup's body."

Sheba drew the canvas back over the face of the dead man. As she followed Macdonald back to the trail, tears filled her eyes. She was remembering that the white, stinging death that had crept upon these men so swiftly had missed her by a hair's breadth. The strong, lusty life had been stricken out of the big Cornishman and probably of his partner in crime. Perhaps they had left mothers or wives or sweethearts to mourn them.

Macdonald relieved Elliot at breaking trail and the young man went back to the gee-pole. They had discarded mukluks and wore moccasins and snowshoes. It was hard, slow work, for the trail-breaker had to fight his way through snow along the best route he could find. The moon was high when at last they reached the roadhouse.

327

CHAPTER XXXII
DIANE CHANGES HER MIND

The news of Sheba's safety had been telephoned to Diane from the roadhouse, so that all the family from Peter down were on the porch to welcome her with mingled tears and kisses. Since Gordon had to push on to the hospital to have Holt taken care of, it was Macdonald who brought the girl home. The mine-owner declined rather brusquely an invitation to stay to dinner on the plea that he had business at the office which would not wait.

Impulsively Sheba held out both her hands to him. "Believe me, I am thanking you with the whole of my heart, my friend. And I'm praying for you the old Irish blessing, 'God save you kindly.'"

The deep-set, rapacious eyes of the Scotchman burned into hers for an instant. Without a word he released her hands and turned away.

Her eyes followed him, a vital, dynamic American who would do big, lawless things to the day of his death. She sighed. He had been a great figure in her life, and now he had passed out of it.

As soon as she was alone with Diane, her Irish

cousin dropped the little bomb she had up her sleeve.

"I'm going to be married Thursday, Di."

Mrs. Paget embraced her for the tenth time within the hour. She was very fond of Sheba, and she had been on a great strain concerning her safety. That out of her danger had resulted the engagement Diane had hoped for was surplusage of good luck.

"You lucky, sensible girl."

Sheba assented demurely. "I do think I'm sensible as well as lucky. It isn't every girl that knows the right man for her even when he wants her. But I know at last. He's the man for me out of ten million."

"I'm sure of it, dear. Oh, I am *so* glad." Diane hugged her again. She couldn't help it.

"One gets to know a man pretty well on a trip like that. I wouldn't change mine for any one that was ever made. I like everything about him, Di. I am the happiest girl."

"I'm so glad you see it that way at last." Diane passed to the practical aspect of the situation. "But Thursday. Will that give us time, my dear? And who are you going to have here?"

"Just the family. I've invited two guests, but neither of them can come. One has a broken leg and the other says he doesn't want to see me married to another man," Sheba explained with a smile.

"So Gordon won't come."

"Yes. He'll have to be here. We can't get along without the bridegroom. It wouldn't be a legal marriage, would it?"

Diane looked at her, for the moment dumb. "You little wretch!" she got out at last. "So it's Gordon, is it? Are you quite sure this time? Not likely to change your mind before Thursday?"

"I suppose, to an outsider, I do seem fickle," Miss O'Neill admitted smilingly. "But Gordon and I both understand that."

"And Colby Macdonald—does he understand it too?"

"Oh, yes." Her smile grew broader. "He told me that he didn't think I would quite suit him, after all. Not enough experience for the place."

Diane flashed a suspicious look of inquiry. "Of course that's nonsense. What did he tell you?"

"Something like that. He will marry Mrs. Mallory, I think, though he doesn't know it yet."

"You mean she will get him on the rebound," said Diane bluntly.

"That isn't a nice way to put it. He has always liked her very much. He is fond of her for what she is. What attracted him in me were the things his imagination gave to me."

"And Gordon likes you, I suppose, for what you are?"

Sheba did not resent the little note of friendly sarcasm. "I suppose he has his fancies about me, too, but by the time he finds out what I am he'll have to put up with me."

The arrival of Elliot interrupted confidences. He had come, he said, to receive congratulations.

"What in the world have you been doing with your face?" demanded Diane. As an afterthought she added: "Mr. Macdonald is all cut up too."

"We've been taking massage treatment." Gordon passed to a subject of more immediate interest. "Do I get my congratulations, Di?"

She kissed him, too, for old sake's sake. "I do believe you'll suit Sheba better than Colby Macdonald would. He's a great man and you are not. But it isn't everybody that is fit to be the wife of a great man."

"That's a double, left-handed compliment," laughed Gordon. "But you can't say anything that will hurt my feelings to-day, Di. Isn't that your baby I hear crying? What a heartless mother you are!"

Diane gave him the few minutes alone with Sheba that his gay smile had asked for. "Get out with you," she said, laughing. "Go to the top of the hill and look at the lovers' moon I've ordered there expressly for you; and while you are there forget that there are going to be crying babies and nursemaids with evenings out in that golden future of yours."

"Come along, Sheba. We'll start now on the golden trail," said Elliot.

She walked as if she loved it. Her long, slender legs moved rhythmically and her arms swung true as pendulums.

The moon was all that Diane had promised. Sheba drank it in happily.

"I believe I must be a pagan. I love the sun and the moon and I know it's all true about the little folk and the pied piper and—"

"If it's paganism to be in love with the world, you are a thirty-third-degree pagan."

"Well, and was there ever a more beautiful night before?"

He thought not, but he had not the words to tell her that for him its beauty lay largely in her presence. Her passionate love of things fine and brave transformed the universe for him. It was enough for him to be near her, to hear the laughter bubbling in her throat, to touch her crisp, blue-black hair as he adjusted the scarf about her head.

"God made the night," he replied. "So that's a Christian thought as well as a pagan one."

They were no exception to the rule that lovers are egoists. The world for them to-night divided itself into two classes. One included Sheba O'Neill and Gordon Elliot; the other took in the uninteresting remnant of humanity. No matter how far afield their talk began, it always came back to themselves. They wanted to know all about each other, to compare experiences and points of view. But time fled too fast for words.

They talked—as lovers will to the end of time—in exclamations and the meeting of eyes and little endearments.

When Diane and Peter found them on the hilltop, Sheba protested, with her half-shy, half-audacious smile, that it could not be two hours since she and Gordon had left the living-room. Peter grinned. He remembered a hilltop consecrated to his own courtship of Diane.

The only wedding present that Macdonald sent Sheba was a long envelope with two documents attached by a clip. One was from the Kusiak "Sun." It announced that the search party had found the body of Northrup with the rest of the stolen gold beside him. The other was a copy of a legal document. Its effect was that the district attorney had dismissed all charges pending against Gordon Elliot.

Although Macdonald lost the coal claims at Kamatlah by reason of the report of Elliot, all Alaska still believes that he was right. In that country of strong men he stands head and shoulders above his fellows. He has the fortunate gift of commanding the admiration of friend and foe alike. The lady who is his wife is secretly the greatest of his slaves, but she tries not to let him know how much he has captured her imagination. For Genevieve Macdonald cannot quite under-stand, herself, how so elemental an emotion as love can have pierced the armor of her sophistication.

Center Point Large Print
600 Brooks Road / PO Box 1
Thorndike, ME 04986-0001 USA

(207) 568-3717

US & Canada:
1 800 929-9108
www.centerpointlargeprint.com